MW00883823

ANNIE'S MONSTER

BOOKS BY

Barbara Corcoran

A Dance to Still Music
The Long Journey
Meet Me at Tamerlaine's Tomb
A Row of Tigers
Sasha, My Friend
A Trick of Light
The Winds of Time
All the Summer Voices
The Clown
Don't Slam the Door When You Go
Sam
This Is a Recording
Axe-Time, Sword-Time
Cabin in the Sky
The Faraway Island
Make No Sound
Hey, That's My Soul You're Stomping On
"Me and You and a Dog Named Blue"
Rising Damp
You're Allegro Dead
A Watery Grave
August, Die She Must
The Woman in Your Life
Mystery on Ice
Face the Music
I Am the Universe
A Horse Named Sky
You Put Up with Me, I'll Put Up with You
The Hideaway
The Sky Is Falling
The Private War of Lillian Adams
The Potato Kid
Annie's Monster

ANNIE'S MONSTER

Barbara Corcoran

A Jean Karl Book

Atheneum New York

COLLIER MACMILLAN CANADA
Toronto

MAXWELL MACMILLAN INTERNATIONAL
PUBLISHING GROUP
New York Oxford Singapore Sydney

to Jeanne

THE TOWN AND THE CHARACTERS IN THIS BOOK ARE ENTIRELY PRODUCTS OF THE AUTHOR'S IMAGINATION.

Atheneum
Macmillan Publishing Company
866 Third Avenue, New York, NY 10022

Collier Macmillan Canada, Inc.
1200 Eglinton Avenue East
Suite 200
Don Mills, Ontario, M3C 3N1

Printed in the United States of America
10 9 8 7 6 5 4 3 2

Library of Congress Cataloging-in-Publication Data
Corcoran, Barbara.
Annie's monster / Barbara Corcoran.—1st ed.
p. cm.
Summary: Thirteen-year-old Annie, living with her family in a small Massachusetts town where her father is an Episcopal minister, is delighted when her prayers for an Irish wolfhound are answered; but she finds herself in more trouble than she bargained for when she tries to deal with the consequences of the large dog's playful curiosity.
ISBN 0-689-31632-1
[1. Dogs—Fiction. 2. Mentally ill—Fiction. 3. Clergy—Fiction. 4. Massachusetts—Fiction.] I. Title.
PZ7.C814An 1990 [Fic]—dc20 89-28121 CIP AC

chapter 1

Annie rode her bike around the parish house for the fourth time, wishing she had a bionic ear so she could hear what was going on. Her father, who was the priest in this Episcopal parish, was attending a meeting of the vestry.

It was not the state of the church's finances she wanted to hear about, nor the ongoing argument over whether they should or should not have an American flag in the church at all times or just on national holidays or never. What she wanted to hear was her father's answer to his young curate, Father Ben, about the dog. And she knew they wouldn't get around to that until the meeting was over and the last of the vestrymen had gone home. It was a personal matter.

But the meeting seemed to drag on and on. She rode up the graveled driveway to the little Gothic fieldstone church, parked her bike, and tried the wooden paneled door. It was kept locked most of the time when the church wasn't in use, but tonight it was open. She pushed it ajar and went inside.

The hush of the church when it was empty always moved her. She went down to one of the pews near the front. The last light of the July evening slanted through the stained-glass window, making the figures glow. She knelt and looked up at the altar.

In her mind she said, "God, I really don't approve of people asking for things, like 'Please let me win the lottery' or 'Please make my wife stop throwing temper tantrums.' With a universe on your hands, you've got enough to do. But if you could see your way clear to having Father say yes to Benny about the dog, I certainly would appreciate it. It's such a stroke of luck—well, such an act of God—that Mrs. Meyers has that wonderful Irish wolfhound that she asked Benny to find a good home for, just because it has a slight flaw in its back knees and can't be a show dog, and Benny wants her to give it to me. But after my cairn died, Father said, 'No more dogs.' He says they make him sneeze, but I would keep an Irish wolfhound outside. It's too big for a house dog. It's the biggest breed in the world, but I guess you know that." She paused and for a moment let herself imagine walking through town with her Irish wolfhound on a splendid red-leather leash. Everybody would say, "What a beautiful dog! What a magnificent creature!"

She shifted her knees on the prayer bench. "But it's not just that I want to show off, God. It's three months since my cairn, Bingo, died, and I miss him so much." She looked up at a sound in the front of the church. Mrs. Ashley, a member of the Altar Guild, had come in with fresh flowers for the altar. She glanced down into the pews and saw Annie. She nodded and smiled approvingly.

Annie got to her feet quickly and went out. She felt guilty, knowing that nice Mrs. Ashley was thinking what a devoted child Father MacDougal's oldest was. Annie could almost hear her saying, "Just think, only thirteen and so dedicated. In church praying all by herself on a Saturday night." Of course she had not been there because she was a good, devoted child but because she desperately wanted that Irish wolfhound.

But she had stayed too long. The cars of the members of the vestry were gone. Even Benny's motorcycle was gone. How could she not have heard it? Only her father's old station wagon was still there. She thought about going into the parish hall and asking him what he had said to Benny's question, but she was too scared. She could imagine him looking at her with those cool blue eyes and saying, "I said no, of course." She rode slowly home. It was crazy to think he would say yes.

chapter 2

When Annie came into the kitchen, her brother Malcolm was finishing off a box of graham crackers and a half gallon of milk.

"You could have left at least one cracker," she said.

"Are you kidding? I'm playing my finals match Monday. I've got to keep my energy up."

"Maybe other people need energy, too."

"For what? Reading books?"

She felt too depressed to argue. Malcolm would win his match, anyway. He'd been junior tennis champion of the county for the last two years. He always won everything. It was he who was supposed to have been the first child, Dougal Andrew MacDougal, Junior. Everyone went into shock when Annie arrived instead. Her parents hadn't even thought about girls' names. So her mother hastily came up with her best friend's name. The real Anne Adair was tall, graceful, and beautiful and acted in Off-Broadway plays, and here was Annie MacDougal, brown haired, gray eyed, short, skinny, and totally untalented.

When Malcolm arrived about a year later, Father had decided against having a Junior. Malcolm grew into the perfect number-one son, good at almost everything.

A year and a half after Malcolm came Robert, who started swimming at the age of three and became almost as famous at the Y swimming pool as Malcolm was on the tennis courts. Robert was also a gifted storyteller.

Finally, three years after Robert, Sherry danced her way into the world. Now eight and a half, she was spending a month at a camp for gifted child dancers. In a family of stars, Annie told herself, I am the black hole.

"Father Benny called you," Malcolm said as he went out the door, swinging his tennis racket.

Annie jumped. "Did he leave a message?"

"Said he'd call later." The screen door slammed.

Benny would have the word about the dog. She ran into the hall and dialed his number, but the answering machine came on: "This is Father Ben's residence. I'm out at the moment, saving the world and all that. If you'll leave your name and number on this infernal machine, I'll get back to you. Wait for the beep . . . the beep . . . the beep . . ."

Annie grinned and waited for the beep. "It's just me," she said, and hung up.

People always commented on the difference between

the very tall, austere, bald Father MacDougal, with his impeccable Oxford accent, and his short, wiry, street-smart curate from South Boston, who rode a motorcycle, played clarinet in a pickup band when he had the time, and loved to shock some of the more shockable parishioners. The two had many ongoing arguments about women priests, the Episcopalian gay-lesbian group, revisions in the prayer book, and social issues. Although they seldom agreed and were often furiously angry with each other, there was a strong mutual respect. The younger church members loved Father Ben.

Annie held her breath as she heard her father's station wagon coming up the street. She looked out the window as if she could read his mind from this distance. He always drove with his back pressed against the seat, his arms held stiff, as if he expected to have to stop the wagon by sheer muscle power. He was not a man who trusted machinery.

She cleaned up the crumbs Malcolm had left and put his glass in the dishwasher. She could hear Robert's computer in his room over the kitchen. He was being tutored to make up a bad grade in math. She was glad his grades were as erratic as hers. Malcolm was a steady *B*-plus student.

She heard the rumble of the garage door closing. The church had offered to install an automatic door opener, but Father MacDougal said the idea of pressing a button as he turned into the drive and seeing the garage door open horrified him. "It's demonism." He was joking, but he did decline the offer.

Annie's mother had wanted the automatic opener for the heavy door, but she didn't argue; she just said, with gentle irony, "Obviously, if the Lord had meant for garage doors to open by themselves, he would have so informed them."

She came into the kitchen in her painting smock with a dab of pink paint on her face. She did rosemaling—painting floral designs on wood—and she was so good at it that she had a steady outlet in the gift shops, and in winter she taught classes.

She was tall. She had once been a hippie, and she still wore her hair in a long ripple down her back, like Rapunzel.

"Hello, dear," she said. "Do I hear your father approaching with his usual stealth?"

Annie laughed. Her father always made a racket opening and closing doors. As his wife told him, he would never have made a success as a cat burglar.

Annie hadn't told her mother about the dog. She knew she would say, "That one is up to your father."

He flung open the door and came in. He was fifteen years older than his wife. He had grown up in Toronto, of Scottish parentage, and been sent to Oxford for his education. After his first wife died, he came to the States. He and Annie's mother had literally bumped into each other in the Boston Public Gardens on a day when she had come to town feeling fed up with her commune in the Berkshires. He took her to tea at the Copley Plaza, and, as she said, she decided then and there that she was putting the life of tofu and granola behind her.

"Good evening, my dear," he said as he came into the kitchen. "Good evening, Daughter."

Annie murmured, "Hello, Father," and held her breath.

"How did the meeting go?" His wife poured his coffee.

He shrugged. "Well enough." He loosened his clerical collar, took off his gray-and-white seersucker jacket, and sat down. "I do get tired of the battle over the flag: Do we or don't we hang it in the church, and when? I was tempted to suggest a Confederate flag as a compromise."

"That would have made a big hit." His wife scooped a spoonful of whipped cream into his coffee.

"Ben and I got into a bit of a row over whether we should provide funds for the soup kitchen at Saint Andrew and All Saints. As if we didn't have enough trouble keeping our own parish solvent. As Ben well knows, I believe in sending our charitable funds to the missions."

"People get hungry here, too, dear. Not just in Africa."

"You always take Ben's side."

"No, but I know what it's like not to have enough to eat. And Ben knows. To you it's an abstraction. You can afford to consider questions like whether it's more self-gratifying to give to people we know . . ."

Annie tuned out the conversation. She'd heard it all many times before. If her father and Ben had had an argument, maybe Ben hadn't even remembered to mention the dog. She headed for the door.

"Annie," her father said.

"Yes, Father?"

"Ben mentioned something about a dog belonging to Mrs. Meyers."

"Yes, Father." She tensed for the refusal.

"Why didn't you speak to me about it yourself?"

For a moment she couldn't think of an answer. "Mrs. Meyers spoke to Father Ben about it. He mentioned it to me, and we thought . . ."

"You thought he might have greater powers of persuasion than you."

She didn't answer. That had been it.

Her father took another sip of coffee and carefully wiped the whipped cream from his lip. The overhead light made his bald head shiny. "It is obviously not a house dog."

A faint hope began to rise. "Ben said he could make a run."

"Pah! Ben thinks he can do everything. I don't want a flimsy homemade job in my yard. If you take the dog, we'll have a proper chain-link fence."

"Yes, Father." Her heart was pounding. He *was* going to say yes!

"It must be understood that you would have complete responsibility for this creature. No disasters like Sherry's kitten."

"What *are* you two talking about?" Annie's mother said.

"Emma Meyers has offered Annie an Irish wolfhound. A very *large* animal."

Annie's mother looked at her. "Well, tell her, Dougal. Is she to have the dog or not?"

"Certainly," he said. "I hope I'm a reasonable man."

"Father!" Annie threw her arms around him.

He disengaged himself. "Come now, let's not get hysterical."

"Thank you very, very, very much! You have answered my prayers."

"Only God can do that. And please remember that this dog is totally your responsibility in every way. Otherwise, back it goes."

"Oh, *yes*," she said. "In every way."

She raced upstairs and dialed Ben's number. This time he answered. "Benny! He said yes!"

"I know. I tried to call you. Listen, I'll come over tomorrow and build a run."

"He's going to buy me a chain-link fence."

Ben whistled, a piercing sound in Annie's ear. "Well, you never know, do you? If he'll be so generous as to let me order it, I know a guy who can get it for you wholesale."

"Don't be mad at Father. I'm sure he'd like to get it wholesale."

Ben laughed. "I'm sure he would."

"Thanks a million times for asking him. He would have said no to me."

"He almost said it to me. But Emma Meyers is not to be treated lightly. She's the biggest contributor we have."

After she had stopped talking to Ben, she knelt by the window in her bedroom and looked up at the sky. The stars had never seemed so bright. "Thanks, God," she said. "Wow! That was a squeaker."

chapter 3

Annie was hoping Mrs. Meyers would be in church so she could talk to her about the dog. She hadn't had a chance to talk again to Ben. She saw him at the front of the church, putting out the wafers and wine for Communion. His vestments always looked slightly too big for him, and his boyish face made visitors mistake him for an altar boy. He had his Sicilian mother's blond hair and his father's brown eyes and sallow skin. People often asked how an Italian kid from South Boston became an Episcopal priest. He had varied answers, depending on who asked, but in fact he had been influenced by an Episcopal priest who had organized a boys' club in his neighborhood when Ben was a teenager.

There were not many people in church on this summer morning. The MacDougals sat in the third pew, as always, but behind them the church was nearly empty.

As the organist began the processional hymn, Annie heard the door close. She turned her head and saw Mrs. Meyers and her eight-year-old daughter come in and sit down near the back. Heads turned discreetly to look. Mrs. Meyers, the wealthiest woman in town and a big contributor to the church, was tall and attractive, and, in Annie's opinion, was one of the friendliest people in the parish. Her daughter had had a freak accident in a badminton game that had caused her to lose an eye. She was very self-conscious about her glass eye. Annie always tried to talk to her, but the child was so shy, she was hard to reach.

The service seemed unusually long. Benny preached the sermon, and she listened carefully. He was talking about the homeless. Sometimes her father complained that Benny was more of a sociologist than a priest, that he cared more about people than he did about the word of God. Benny always answered, "If the word of God isn't meant for people, who is it meant for?" They had long arguments that sometimes seemed pointless to Annie.

When church was finally over, Annie hurried out to speak to Mrs. Meyers. She wanted to thank her for the dog and to find out anything she ought to know about him.

Mrs. Meyers took Annie's hand in both of hers. "I'm so glad you're going to have him. Benny told me about your losing your little cairn. We know how that feels, don't we, Harriet?" She smiled at her daughter, who was standing close to her mother. Harriet nodded.

"I'll take good care of him," Annie said.

"We know you will. He's almost a year old, so he should be calming down soon. An Irish pup is a handful. They're so darned big."

"He knocks me down," Harriet said, smiling shyly at Annie.

"How do you like that?" Annie tried not to be conscious of the child's one immovable eye. Harriet was a pretty girl but for that eye.

"I don't mind. He doesn't mean to."

"Annie," Mrs. Meyers said, "I'll write out his diet and all that." She rummaged in her purse for a card and scribbled a number on it. "This is the kennel number and this is the house. Call me if you have any questions. I told Ben you can have one of my prefab doghouses; I have more than I'm using." She nodded to three women who were standing near, obviously eavesdropping. "Good morning, Mrs. Evans . . . Mrs. Parsons . . . Mrs. uh . . ." She slid past the name of the third woman, which she obviously had forgotten. "Beautiful day. Lovely sermon."

They answered enthusiastically, happy to be spoken to by the richest woman in town.

Mrs. Meyers turned back to Annie. "He'll be at the vet's for a few days, getting shots and being neutered. Since he has that fault with his hocks, I can't breed him, and I don't want him running around knocking up every bitch in heat." She looked at the three women again as one of them gasped. She laughed. "We're talking about one of my dogs. Bitches in heat isn't proper language for the churchyard if one is referring to people, is it? But it's just dog talk."

The women smiled politely, and Mrs. Evans, whose

face reminded Annie of Silly Putty, said, "We understand."

Annie knew they would have plenty to say to one another later. She had heard them often. They were nice enough women in their way, but they loved to gossip, especially about Mrs. Meyers, probably because she had all that money, and maybe partly because she spoke her mind.

Mrs. Meyers gave Annie a pat as Annie thanked her once more for the dog. "It's Flanagan's good luck. His registered name, by the way, is Ian Flanagan of Wild Rose Farm, but call him whatever you want." She turned away to talk to Annie's mother.

"You can come see Ian Flanagan whenever you want to," Annie said to Harriet.

Harriet gave her a shy smile. "Thank you."

Annie watched her go off to the car with her mother, thinking how a crazy accident like the one that ruined Harriet's eye could probably change your whole life, no matter how much money your family had.

Robert caught up with her as she started to walk home. "Did you pray for Mal to win his championship tomorrow?"

"No. He'll win."

"What if we prayed for him and the other kid's family prayed for him? What a spot to put God in."

"How come you're looking so cheerful today?"

"I'm a cheerful type. But three good things happened. Mrs. Daniels asked me to give her kids swimming lessons in their new pool. They know how to swim, she says, but they keep sinking."

Annie laughed. "What else good?"

"I figured out a math problem that I've been fighting

for three days. Mr. Bullis is going to faint." Mr. Bullis was his tutor.

"And?"

"This is the best: Mrs. Francis sent me a notice about a publishing company that gives a prize for the best book by a kid under twelve. If I can finish it before my birthday, I can send something."

"You'll win."

"Come on. I haven't even got an idea yet. But I can take a whack at it. I've got three months and four days."

So Rob would be busy for the rest of the summer, and Malcolm would be playing tennis every day, and Sherry was at the dance camp. Well, she was going to have a project herself. Ian Flanagan of Wild Rose Farm—her dog, her art, her craft, her sport, all rolled into one.

chapter 4

"The hardware store will deliver the chain-link panels this afternoon," her father said. "Just make sure Ben puts them together properly. And remember, at least fifty feet from the Anderson property. I don't want any more hassles with Jack Anderson. The town clerk said fifty feet is the ordinance."

"We'll make it fifty-two, just to be sure," Annie said.

"At least it will be a few yards of lawn that won't require mowing," her father said.

Their neighbors, the Andersons, were suspicious, unfriendly people who delighted in starting bitter arguments.

They were elderly, childless, and petless. Jack Anderson had run for the board of selectmen eleven times and had been defeated eleven times. "Not only defeated," her father always said, "but last."

He went off to make some calls. Robert had gone to give swimming lessons, Malcolm for a last warm-up before his match, and her mother had gone to Rockport to deliver some of her rosemaled trays and baskets to the gift shops.

Annie went to the back of their property and carefully measured fifty-two feet from the spirea hedge that marked the border between the Anderson property and theirs. She drove a pair of stakes into the ground and stretched a piece of string from one to the other. Just as she finished, a sound on the other side of the hedge made her look up.

"Just what are you doing now?" Mr. Anderson was scowling, as usual.

She wanted to say, I made a model of your heart and I'm driving a stake through it. I'm a witch. But she actually said, "I'm marking off fifty-two feet from the property line."

"What for?"

"We're putting up a run for my dog."

"I thought your dog died."

"I'm getting a new one." And how do you like that, Mr. Sourpuss?

He wagged his finger at her. "If this animal barks or makes a nuisance or comes on my land, I'll report it."

"Mr. Anderson," she said, "all dogs bark sometimes."

"I won't put up with an annoyance right under my windows. Ordinance fifty-three clearly states that unnecessary and annoying noise is prohibited. And if I have my way, we'll soon have a leash law. It's shameful the way dogs run loose in this town." He stalked off toward his house.

Annie watched him. He and his wife looked more and more alike as they got older. They reminded her of a ceramic salt-and-pepper shaker set she had seen in a gift shop, designed to look like two square, squat figures. She wished they would move away, but they never would.

She tried to concentrate on her dog to get Mr. Anderson out of her mind. What would he be like? Ben said that Mrs. Meyers told him Irish wolfhounds were gentle and affectionate. She had seen one with Mrs. Meyers a few times in the kennel's station wagon, but she hadn't seen one up close. They were the biggest breed of dogs, and Flanagan was eleven months old, so he would be almost full-grown.

She went into the house and made herself a sandwich. The conversation between her mother and father the night before came back to her mind. She had been so nervous, waiting for her father's verdict about the dog, she hadn't paid much attention. Her mother had said she knew what it was like to be hungry. Her family had been poor, but Annie hadn't realized they had been that poor. They had all died, parents and a brother, before her mother even met Annie's father.

She bit into her peanut-butter-and-raspberry-jam sandwich, trying to imagine what it would be like to be hungry, not just for an hour or so but for days, maybe even all the time, like the children in Third World countries. She decided she would give Benny her allowance, or most of it, to give to that soup kitchen at Saint Andrew's.

Robert came home, his curly brown hair slicked down from swimming.

"How'd it go?"

"Okay. Mrs. Daniels made me show her how you save somebody from drowning, and when I showed her my lifesaving certificate, she put on her glasses and read every word. But after that she took off, and we got along all right. That Ruthie's kind of a slow learner." Unlike his brother, Robert was short and compactly built. He took off his glasses and rubbed his eyes. "Chlorine. I stink of chlorine. Yuk." He ate a sandwich and went upstairs to shower.

Benny and the man from the hardware store arrived within minutes of each other. Robert and Annie helped the man unload the posts and the chain-link segments, and he showed Benny how to put them together. In a shorter time than Annie had imagined, the run was completed.

Benny mopped his sweating face with the sleeve of his T-shirt, looking like the street kid he had been, in his faded jeans, sneakers with no socks, and a red headband to keep his floppy blond hair out of his eyes.

While he was hanging the gate, both of the Andersons appeared.

"That thing is an eyesore," Mr. Anderson said. "It may be illegal. Did you get permission from the planning board?"

"My father did," Annie said.

"What kind of dog needs a huge run like that?" Mrs. Anderson demanded.

Benny answered. "He's an Irish wolfhound. They're

pretty big dogs." He took a swallow from the bottle of Coke Robert had brought him. "Fine dogs."

Mr. Anderson sneered. "I suppose where you come from, you're familiar with pedigreed dogs."

Benny turned toward him quickly, swinging the Coke bottle gently back and forth. "Where I come from, sir," he said softly, "we have mutts, and they're scroungy and half-starved and mean."

Mr. Anderson backed away, keeping his eye on the bottle in Benny's hand.

"Don't you dare threaten my husband!" Mrs. Anderson said.

"Why, Mrs. Anderson, what an idea!" Benny turned his back on them and finished hanging the gate.

Robert laughed.

The Andersons marched off to their house, indignation showing in every step.

"That was a neat put-down," Robert said.

Ben grinned, showing his even white teeth and the dimple at the corner of his mouth. "Put-down? Who, me? I always respect my elders."

"Oh, sure," Robert said.

"What if Flanagan does bark?" Annie said. "Like at night?"

"Annie, half the dogs in this town bark at night. I'm an insomniac, and believe me, I know. There's no law against it. Anyway, they're so sick of Jack Anderson's complaints at the town hall, they hide when they see him coming."

"I'm going over to the courts to watch Malcolm win his match," Robert said. "See ya later." He got on his bike and took off.

"And I've got a band rehearsal with the kids at the home." At least once a week Benny drove twelve miles to a home for retarded boys, to give them music lessons. It was one of the things he and Annie's father argued about. Her father thought Benny should not take that time away from his parish work. Annie was on Benny's side. She had gone there once when the boys gave a concert for their families, and she had seen how much it meant to them. Sometimes Robert went with Ben and played what he called his feeble harmonica.

She watched Benny take off on his motorcycle. It would have felt lonesome with everyone gone, but the presence of the dog run was too exciting. She got the food dish and the water dish that had been Bingo's and took them out to the run. Mrs. Meyers hadn't said for sure when Flanagan would come. It depended on how long he had to stay at the vet's. She hoped he wouldn't feel sick. It must be kind of traumatic, she thought, to be neutered. Bingo had been neutered, though, and it hadn't slowed him down any. Handling his dishes made her miss him again.

"Bingo," she said aloud, "I'll never forget you, no matter how much I like the new dog."

chapter 5

In the afternoon Annie rode her bike out to Ames's meadow to look it over. She hadn't been there for a while, but it seemed like the best place to give Flanagan his exercise and his obedience training. She had taken Bingo to obedience school, so she knew something about how to train a dog to sit and heel and obey simple commands.

She was beginning to feel nervous about Flanagan. What if he didn't like her? What if he turned out not to be good-natured after all? A dog that big would be impossible to manage if he chose not to be managed.

When she got home, the family members were gathered in the living room, as they often were late in the day.

It was a ritual with her father to have one glass of sherry while her mother had a cup of tea, and the children had weak tea or a cold drink, if they wanted it.

She sensed the tension in the room as soon as she came in. Her father was standing in his familiar pose, his back to the stone fireplace, one elbow on the mantel. Her mother was pouring tea. Robert sprawled on the sofa drinking a Coke, and Malcolm sat stiffly on the edge of the only uncomfortable chair in the room. He looked miserable.

"What's the matter?" Annie said.

"Your brother is no longer county champion," her father said.

Annie's mother frowned. "You don't have to put it quite so brutally, Dougal."

"When you want very much to win, losing is brutal," her husband answered. "Why indulge in euphemisms and evasions?"

Annie could hardly believe he was saying what she thought he was saying. "You don't mean you lost, do you?" she said to Malcolm.

He shot her a look. "When you don't win, that usually means you lost."

"But you never lose."

"This time he did," her father said. "And I hope he is sportsman enough not to go into a decline over it."

Annie couldn't think why her father was being so unsympathetic, but then it occurred to her that he was probably almost as disappointed as Malcolm was. He liked his children to shine in whatever they did.

"You'll win next year," Annie said.

"This may wreck my chances for the Davis Cup tryouts," Malcolm said.

"Malcolm dear," his mother said, "you're young. Time enough to catch up again."

"Coach says I blew it." Malcolm looked close to tears.

"Oh, him," Robert said. "He always says things like that. That's his idea of psyching you up."

"It doesn't seem to have worked," their father said dryly.

"Mal played just fine," Robert said. "The other guy was a real superman, that's all. He had a serve like a cannonball."

"Dinner in twenty-five minutes," their mother said. "If you're all going to shower, you'd better get started."

Malcolm got up. "I'm not hungry." He started out of the room.

"Nevertheless, you will come to dinner," his father said. "One of the rules in this house is that we eat on time, and everyone is there."

Also, Annie thought, one of us is supposed to have a topic of general interest for discussion. They took turns, and it was Malcolm's turn, but they were allowed to exchange if they wanted to. She followed Malcolm out of the room. "I'll take the topic if you don't want to do it."

He nodded and ran upstairs. Robert followed him. Annie started back to the living room to tell her father she would do the topic, but she stopped near the door. Her mother was talking.

"You weren't very kind, Dougal."

"The boy has to learn how to lose. It's not winning or losing that counts, it's . . ."

His wife interrupted him. " . . . it's how you play the game. That wretched prep-school slogan. The child is used to winning. It hurt to lose."

"Then let him take it like a man."

"Oh, bull!" she said. "If we'd had you in our commune twenty years ago, we'd have knocked that stiff-upper-lip stuff out of you."

Annie held her breath, expecting him to lose his temper. Nobody but her mother dared talk to him like that.

But he laughed. "You're outrageous," he said. "But I suppose that's why I married you."

Annie headed for the stairs, not wanting them to discover she had overheard them.

In her room she flipped through her encyclopedia looking for a dinner topic. It was supposed to be a statement or a question that would provoke discussion. Usually her father did most of the discussing.

She thought of a quotation her science teacher had told the class: Einstein had said, "God doesn't play at dice." She couldn't remember what it referred to, but never mind, it would start something.

While her father carved the roast, she brought up her subject.

Robert dived right in. He amazed her, the strange things he knew, like the speed of light, and what protons and neutrons were.

Father came at the subject from the theological point of view, and he and Robert had a lively argument about the Big Bang theory.

Malcolm was silent, pushing his food around on his plate and eating little. His eyes were red.

"What are your thoughts on this, Malcolm?" his father asked.

Malcolm shook his head. "I don't know." He stared at his plate.

"None of us can *know*," his father said, "unless one of us can read the mind of God. I asked what you think."

"I guess I don't think anything about it, Father." Malcolm took a shaky breath and looked at his mother. "May I be excused?"

Before she could answer, his father said, "No, you may not. We don't jump up from the table at our whim. A meal is a ceremony, for which we have given thanks to God."

"Dougal," his wife said hastily, "have some more asparagus. Fresh from May Sheldon's garden."

Annie felt sorry for Malcolm. Father could be a tyrant. She watched Malcolm try to eat some asparagus and knew how it felt trying to swallow past the tears in your throat. She wondered if Father had been a perfect child.

After a glance at Robert, Annie and he began asking Father a lot of questions, about Genesis and other biblical accounts, trying to get his attention away from Malcolm. All four of them had learned that trick to protect one another. Annie wished Sherry were there, because she was a natural chatterer, and she was best at diverting Father.

When it was time for dessert, the discussion always ended. Now they could talk about anything. Annie gave them a vivid account of the building of the dog run and the reactions of the Andersons, talking as she and Robert cleared the dishes and began to bring in the dessert.

"You may be excused now, Malcolm," their father said.

"Oh, Dougal!" His wife looked distressed. "It's strawberry shortcake."

"If the boy doesn't eat his normal meal, he doesn't get dessert. That's one of life's inflexible rules. You may go to your room now, Malcolm."

Malcolm shoved his chair back, burst into tears, and ran upstairs. The rest of them ate their dessert in silence. It was delicious, but Annie hardly tasted it, she was so angry with her father.

Later in the evening when her parents were watching TV, Annie fixed a big bowl of strawberry shortcake and took it up to Malcolm's room. She knocked; when he didn't answer, she opened the door and went in, anyway. He was lying on his bed, face to the wall.

"Secret dessert," she said, and put it on the floor beside the bed. "I'm sorry you lost, but you'll win next time. Sometimes Father is a fascist tyrant." Malcolm didn't answer, but that was okay. She knew he'd been crying, and he wouldn't want to let her see that he had.

About half an hour later she heard quiet steps in the hall. She opened her door a crack and saw Robert carrying a bowl of strawberry shortcake to Malcolm's room. She grinned. Her brothers were a pain in the neck sometimes, but when you got right down to the nitty-gritty, they were all right.

chapter 6

He was coming! Ian Flanagan of Wild Rose Farm was coming at 10:30 A.M. Mrs. Meyers had called the night before to say she was bringing him.

"Tommy is coming with me," she said, "to put up the doghouse. It's prefab and it takes only a few minutes."

Mr. Thompson was the man who took care of Mrs. Meyers's kennels. His granddaughter was in Annie's class at school.

From breakfast time on, Annie looked out the window every time she heard a car. She was both excited and scared. What if Flanagan didn't like her? What if he was homesick?

Malcolm and Robert were hanging around the kitchen, too, getting in their mother's way as she made pies with cherries a parishioner had brought.

Their father had gone on his weekly visit to a rest home, where he gave Holy Communion to his parishioners there.

"Would you all please go somewhere else before I fall over you and ruin these pies?" their mother said.

The boys went out in the backyard and tossed a basketball back and forth. Annie sat on the front steps, where she could see cars coming from either direction. It was eleven minutes before ten.

What if they had a wreck on the way? She had a vivid picture of some idiot smashing into them. She got up and paced up and down the sidewalk.

When the car came around the corner and headed toward her house, she thought she was imagining it. But there it was, the blue Volvo wagon with the big dog-cage in back, Mrs. Meyers driving, Mr. Thompson looking small beside her, and Ian Flanagan himself in the cage, his feet braced.

Mrs. Meyers gave a merry toot on the horn and parked neatly in the driveway. Annie's brothers and her mother rushed out to greet the dog, and Annie raced toward the tailgate, wanting to be the first one he saw, in case dogs attached themselves to the first person they saw, the way baby ducks did.

Mr. Thompson got out and opened the cage door, picked up Flanagan's leash, and said, "Out you get, boy."

Flanagan leaped out so suddenly he jerked the leash out of Mr. Thompson's hands. He looked as big as a bear. He put his huge paws on Annie's shoulders. She staggered backward under his weight and sat down hard on the grass. He stood over her and gave her a wet, slurpy kiss on the cheek. For a moment she was frightened; she felt helpless. Then Mr. Thompson pulled him off, and Mrs. Meyers was helping her up.

"What an entrance!" Mrs. Meyers said. "Are you all right, Annie?"

"I'm fine." She felt a little shaky. Flanagan was watching her, wagging his tail. Suddenly she laughed. He was just a great, big baby, with certainly the biggest head she had ever seen on a dog, his amber eyes eager, waiting to see what would happen next.

"That was a bad dog, Flanagan," Mrs. Meyers said. "Bad dog."

"He didn't mean to be bad," Annie said. She put her hand on the rough gray fur of his neck.

"I know, but he's too big to jump on people." She took the dog's head between her hands. "I'm going to miss you, you silly dog. But don't spoil him, Annie. Be firm with him."

Mr. Thompson was unloading the parts of the doghouse.

"Help Mr. Thompson, boys," their mother said. And to Mrs. Meyers she said, "Come in and have some coffee."

"I'd love to. And I have Annie's papers here—owner's registration, license, vet's papers, all that. I'll leave them in the house, Annie."

Mr. Thompson handed the leash to Annie with a grin. "He's yours now. Better get acquainted."

While her mother and Mrs. Meyers went into the house, and Mr. Thompson and the boys went to work erecting the doghouse, Annie stood looking at her dog. He stood quietly, looking at her.

"Hello," she said. "They said you'd be big, but I had no idea." It wasn't just that he was so tall, he was big all over, his square head, his broad shoulders, his well-muscled legs. "You aren't going to grow much more, are you?" she said. "You'd be as big as I am." Tentatively she touched the top of his head, stroking the coarse gray coat.

Gently he tucked his head under her arm. All her hesitation vanished.

"Oh, Flanagan," she said. "We *are* going to be good friends." She hugged him.

chapter 7

Annie went out four times before going to bed, reassuring herself that Flanagan was comfortable and wasn't lonesome. His large, pale blue doghouse looked nice. She took an old quilt out to put on the ground inside the house so he could lie down and feel cozy.

Her father was making a cup of tea when she came in the last time. He looked tired. "Let the dog be, Annie," he said. "If you spoil him, he'll be unmanageable."

"Do you like him, Father?"

"I hardly know him yet."

"I hope he won't make you sneeze, the way Bingo did."

"Oh, I daresay he will. I have an allergy, it seems."

The telephone rang, and he answered it wearily. He was always depressed after he visited old people in the rest home.

"Ben," he said on the phone, "what is it now?" He listened for a moment, then sighed. "Johnny Evans again. Yes, you handle it. You're the one who's good with the druggies. My own impulse is to shake them till their teeth rattle." He listened a minute longer. "Righto." He hung up, shaking his head. "Poor Mrs. Evans. She doesn't deserve those boys."

Annie went upstairs. Malcolm's stereo was playing rock as loudly as he dared when his father was home. Robert was working away on his computer. She went into her room and shut the door, sitting by the window, where she could see the dark outline of Flanagan's run. She hoped he would sleep well.

In bed images ran through her mind: Flanagan on his red leash walking proudly through town, admired by everyone; Flanagan racing across Ames's meadows through the chest-high grass and wildflowers; Flanagan heeling obediently as they explored the paths of the arboretum. "That's Annie MacDougal's dog," everybody would say. "Isn't he a beauty?"

Her digital clock said ten minutes of three when she awoke. She lay still, wondering what had waked her. Then she heard it: a deep-throated bark. Flanagan, no! It stopped and then began again. If he woke the Andersons, they'd complain. She jumped out of bed, grabbed her bathrobe, and ran down the back stairs and let herself out the kitchen door.

The grass felt damp under her bare feet as she ran across the lawn. Flanagan barked once more. It was the deepest bark she had ever heard. Hastily she unlatched the gate to the run, talking to him in a low voice.

"What's the matter, Flanagan? Hush, don't bark." She held out her hand to let him know who she was. He sniffed her fingers and then wagged his tail and pushed his head against her. Something rustled nearby in the hedge. "What was it? A dog? A squirrel? Maybe that raccoon that's been messing around the trash cans." In the darkness she couldn't see anything. She didn't think it was a dog; dogs were more visible. Maybe it was the Ainsleys' cat. She sat down beside Flanagan, patting him. Benny had dumped some cedar chips on the grass in the run. "Your run smells like Mother's cedar chest, where she keeps the blankets," she told him.

He lay down beside her, resting his head in her lap.

"You mustn't bark, especially in the middle of the night. The Andersons would just love an excuse to call the police." The town's police force consisted of Chief Porter and two part-time deputies, Bill Nye and Henry Sullivan. Annie knew them well, as she knew everybody in town, and she liked them, especially tall, burly Chief Porter. She had heard the policemen's opinions of Jack Anderson and his complaints, but still they had to listen.

"I know dogs at a kennel bark whenever they feel like it, but see, this isn't a kennel. This is a private house. It's the rectory. We have to be above reproach—that's what Father is always saying. Not that we are, but we have to try a little harder than other people so Father won't have to take the heat." She glanced toward the house and noticed that no lights had come on. "So you have to be the dog above reproach." She scratched behind his floppy ear. "Are you homesick? Do you miss the other dogs? Was your mother still there at Mrs. Meyers's?"

Flanagan looked at her with his large eyes as if he understood everything she said.

"I've got to go back to bed now," Annie said. "Why don't you go into your nice house and get some sleep? Tomorrow I'll take you for a long walk and show you off."

The front panel of the doghouse was hinged so it could be opened wide in warm weather. Annie opened it as far as it would go.

"There's lots of room in here, and it's airy and nice. Tomorrow I'll find another old quilt or something to put on the floor so you'll be really comfy." She guided him into the house. "Lie down now and go to sleep."

Obediently he lay down, but as soon as she started to leave, he followed her to the gate. She decided she should just go, not talk to him anymore. But as she walked away, he gave his deep bark again.

"Oh, *Flanagan*!" she said. If she went back, he would think he could get her to come to him just by barking. She walked slowly away, but he barked again. In her ears it sounded as loud as thunder; she was sure it could be heard all over town.

A light came on in the house. Luckily it was Robert's room, but if Flanagan had awakened Robert, it wouldn't be long before her father woke up, too, and he would be annoyed. Not to mention the Andersons and the other neighbors. She went back into the run, and Flanagan immediately lay down at her feet.

"All right, I'll stay a few minutes, but this can't go on," she told him. "Tomorrow we've got to have a long talk about this. If you're going to be a public nuisance, I won't be able to keep you, and I couldn't *stand* that." She found a relatively soft grassy place and lay down, wrapping her bathrobe around her. "Lie down and go to sleep." She would wait till he was asleep and then she'd go back to bed.

It was the sun shining in her eyes that woke her. She had slept away what was left of the night. As soon as she stirred, Flanagan bounded to his feet, ready for a game. She got up stiffly, cramped from sleeping on the ground. As much to ease her own muscles as to please Flanagan, she ran with him up and down the run a few times. "Now." She put her hand around his muzzle. "I'm going to shower and have breakfast, and then we'll go for a walk. Don't bark! That's an order."

He watched her wistfully, but he didn't bark. As she was crossing the lawn, her bathrobe trailing, she looked up and saw Mrs. Anderson staring at her from the other side of the hedge.

"Good morning," Annie said brightly. "Lovely day." And she went on to the house trying not to look as if she were hurrying.

chapter 8

You should have taken your sleeping bag." Robert was the only one up.

"I didn't intend to spend the night in the kennel. I fell asleep."

"He's a neat dog."

"I just hope he isn't going to bark all night." She showered and dressed quickly, ate a fast breakfast, and went out to get Flanagan. She could hardly wait to walk him through town. She wished her three best friends weren't away at camp, so she could show him off to them.

Flanagan made small woofing sounds in his throat when he saw her coming.

"We're going out to Ames's meadow," she told him. "You'll like it."

Flanagan trotted beside her, his head held high, his body quivering with energy. When they came out onto the sidewalk, he found dozens of things to explore: flattened pop cans, the end of an ice-cream cone, a butterfly that he leaped at. Several times he almost pulled the leash out of Annie's hand. She realized he had probably spent most of his time in the kennels at the Meyerses' place.

"Do you feel free?" she said. "That's good, but you have to be nice and dignified when we walk through town. Heel, Flanagan."

He heeled instantly, but a moment later he leaped to the top of the stone wall in pursuit of a chipmunk, almost jerking Annie off her feet.

"Flanagan!" She pulled him back and made him sit. "Listen. Wait till we get to the meadow. Then you can chase everything. But in town you have to mind. Got it?" She bent down and looked into his eyes. He seemed to be listening attentively. "Fun is fun, but Mrs. Meyers said 'be firm.' Now. Heel."

The pharmacist drove by and beeped his horn. He pointed at Flanagan and grinned.

Mrs. Altman, the librarian and the church organist, was in her yard feeding her chickens. Annie took an extra-tight grip on the leash as Flanagan showed signs of intense interest.

"My goodness," Mrs. Altman said. "What a fine dog. I hope he doesn't chase chickens."

"Oh, no, I wouldn't let him," Annie said, but she didn't linger to chat.

Farther down the street the gardener at the historical

society house said, "Say! That's a dog and a half. Mind, you keep him out of the flower beds."

"Oh, I will." Annie held the leash in both hands as Flanagan showed signs of wanting to leap into the geraniums.

Ahead of them a group of small children were playing with a ball on the sidewalk. A toddler lurched among them, yelling happily and trying to reach for the ball.

Annie was diverted by the sight of Todd Bethel coming up the street. Todd was one of her heroes. He had just graduated from high school and was going to Bates College in the fall. He'd been captain of the baseball team, and he was an acolyte in her father's church. Sometimes he talked to her, but if he was with other people his own age, he just gave her a remote "Hi."

One of the children threw the ball wildly over the heads of the others. A boy leaped for it and missed. Flanagan gave a joyous woof, jerked free of Annie, and caught the ball in his mouth, dashing into the midst of the children, ready to play the game. Suddenly there was total confusion. Two children crashed into each other and fell down, a little girl began to scream, and Flanagan brushed against the toddler and knocked her off her feet. All the children were shrieking and sobbing. With the ball still in his mouth, Flanagan turned and looked at Annie as if to say, "Why don't they play the game right?"

She caught hold of his leash and pulled him away from the children. He dropped the ball, and it rolled into the gutter. Todd Bethel was picking up the wailing toddler, and the daughter-in-law of Mr. Hanson, who owned the ice-cream parlor, was rushing out of her house to rescue her children.

Annie stuttered apologies as Mrs. Hanson sorted out the children who were hers, the toddler and a four-year-old, her face red with anger and alarm. ". . . no business letting a monster like that . . . report to the police . . ." were some of the words Annie heard as she tried to explain that Flanagan was really friendly.

Mrs. Hanson snatched the little one from Todd's arms, said "Ha!," grabbed the four-year-old by the hand, and marched up the walk to her house. Annie could see doors opening. The other children ran to their houses, terrorized.

Todd and Annie looked at each other.

"That's some dog," Todd said.

Annie was shaking. "He really is . . . I mean, he wouldn't hurt a fly." Her voice trembled.

Todd studied both Annie and Flanagan. Then he patted the dog. "I believe it. Come on, I'll buy you both an ice-cream cone. That was kind of traumatic. Little kids can really scream when they put their minds to it."

She remembered he was an only child. "Yes," she said, "they can."

Todd turned around, and they walked back the way he had come. "He's an Irish wolfhound, isn't he?"

"Yes. Thank you for helping out."

"My pleasure. What kind of ice cream does he like?"

Annie wished she were not so tongue-tied. All she could think of to say was, "I don't know. I've only had him one day."

Todd laughed. "What's his name?"

"Ian Flanagan of Wild Rose Farm."

"Wow, that's elegant." He went into Mr. Hanson's ice-cream store.

Annie moved along out of sight. Mr. Hanson was the father-in-law of the woman whose children Flanagan had just upset. Maybe she'd already told him about it. She'd looked mad enough to tell the whole town.

Todd came out with three double-deckers. "I got Ian Flanagan honey vanilla." He handed Annie a chocolate-almond cone, lapped his own to keep it from dripping on his hand, and offered Flanagan his.

Flanagan sniffed it cautiously and then swallowed it in one gulp.

Todd laughed. "Well, see ya. He's a fine dog." He started back the way he had been going.

"Thank you," Annie called after him. "Very much."

"I told Mr. Hanson what happened," he said, "in case his daughter-in-law gives him some cockamamie story."

"What did he say?"

"He just grinned."

She watched him walk away in his swinging lope. He walked as if he felt good about himself. That must be nice.

She walked Flanagan through the business block without any more trouble.

Past the town limits, Annie ran with Flanagan, trying to keep him down to her pace and pulling him back when he started to break into a gallop.

They cut across the baseball field and up a dirt road with only three houses on it. At the end of the road they climbed the stone wall.

"Behold," she said to him, "Ames's meadow. Look at the wildflowers, blooming just for you." She unsnapped his leash. "Race you to the brook."

When they reached the brook, Flanagan splashed into the shallow water, throwing up a spray that drenched her shirt. She took off her sneakers and went in after him. He gulped down some of the cold water and leaped ahead of her. She threw sticks for him to chase and laughed at him when he brought back the wrong one.

When they had played for a while, she worked with him on obedience. He understood her commands, but he was impatient. When she told him to stay and walked away from him, seconds later he would come trotting after her. But she went through the routines over and over, until he decided it would be fun to obey, like a new game.

Finally she hugged him and said, "Enough for today. You're going to be fine."

It was lunchtime when they got home. "I don't know about you," she said, "but I am beat. Not to mention starved." She gave him a handful of Doggy Treats and left him lying contentedly on the grass.

Her father was beginning to mow the lawn. It was always a grim business. The sitting mower had cost so much her father wouldn't let anyone else touch it, but as Benny said, "If anybody could wreck it, it would be Dougal."

He always dressed for the occasion in an old pair of black pants and a black sweatshirt, no matter how hot the day. It was as if he went into mourning for the grass, Annie thought. He wore a black cloth-visored cap, the kind that comes from feed-and-grain stores, with the visor pulled way down on his forehead to protect him from sunburn. It was understood that he was not to be called to the house for the phone or anything short of impending death. No one breathed easily until the ordeal was over.

Annie scooted into the house as fast as she could, keeping out of his way. She hoped Flanagan wouldn't be frightened. At least the mower made so much noise, he wouldn't be heard if he barked.

Her mother was in the kitchen drinking coffee. Annie got herself some blueberry muffins and a glass of milk. "I may as well tell you," she said to her mother.

Her mother, who was keeping an anxious eye on the mower, said, "When you begin that way, it has to be a disaster of some kind."

"Not really." She told her about the encounter with the children, about young Mrs. Hanson's anger, about Todd's help and what he had told Mr. Hanson.

"Well," her mother said, "you're going to have to keep him away from populated places until he's a little older and more sedate."

"I will."

"Mrs. Meyers came by. They're going to Maine for a month, but Mr. Thompson will be at the kennel if you need advice." She went to the closet where the boys kept baseball and basketball equipment and hockey sticks and brought back a brightly colored ball. "This belongs to Flanagan. Harriet remembered to send it to him. She says it's his favorite toy."

Malcolm charged into the kitchen, swinging his tennis racket. "Hey, guess what!" He was wearing white shorts. His long legs were deeply tanned. "The Y is going to have a tournament at the end of August. I get to play Ned again, and this time I'm going to beat the tar out of him. My picture will be in the *Chronicle* tomorrow."

"Darling, you sound so bloodthirsty," his mother said.

"You bet. I'm out for blood." He grabbed a bottle of Coke and started for the stairs. "I'm going to mangle him!"

"The simple joys of childhood," his mother murmured.

She winced as the lawn mower roared past the kitchen windows.

"He'll scare Flanagan," Annie said. She peered out the windows toward the dog run. "He's running up and down."

Robert came into the kitchen, his hair plastered wet to his head and his swim trunks draped over his shoulder. "I see Father is dealing with Nature again. Your dog doesn't like it."

"Oh, Saint Teresa preserve us, bring him in." Annie's mother looked hot and tired and, as she often described herself, frazzled.

Annie looked startled. "Bring Father in?"

Her mother collapsed into a chair, laughing. "No, no, no. Flanagan."

"Really?" Annie hadn't dreamed she'd be allowed to bring Flanagan into the house for any reason.

"Robert, you go upstairs and shower or something. Let's cut down the crowd factor."

"Why? I want to see Flanagan. He's not some kind of sacred cow, is he?"

His mother fanned herself with her apron. "All right, I see your point, but no games. Put the dog's ball away for now."

Annie threw the ball into the closet and ran out to get Flanagan before her mother changed her mind. She heard her calling, "He *is* housebroken, isn't he?" And she yelled back, "Yes." Mr. Thompson had said he was.

She flew down the driveway, passing close by her father, who was so absorbed he didn't even see her. His face was pink, and his mouth was set in a determined line. He went too fast in the machine, especially when he made one of his swooping turns.

Flanagan pressed against the gate, keeping an eye on the mower. Annie took him back to the house quickly while her father was at the other end of the lawn.

In the kitchen Flanagan sat, as Annie told him to, and looked around the kitchen, taking everything in. Then softly he said, "Woof." Annie's mother and Robert laughed.

"He's given us his approval," her mother said.

Malcolm came downstairs, showered and changed, and rumpled Flanagan's rough coat.

"Gently," his mother said. "Let's don't get him into too playful a mood in the house."

A new roar joined the racket of the lawn mower.

"Benny," Robert said.

His mother turned on the burner under the glass coffeepot.

Benny came in and laughed. "You're hiding from the lawn mower. You look like people in an air-raid shelter. Hello, Flanagan. We meet at last." He held out his hand, and Flanagan laid one large paw in it. "What's this I hear about Flanagan attacking innocent, helpless little children?"

"You've heard already?" Annie was dismayed. Was it going to turn into a big problem?

"I'm always the first to know, especially if it's trouble."

"*Is* it trouble?" Annie's mother asked.

"What are you guys talking about?" Malcolm asked.

"It sounds as if the Bethel kid saved the day. What exactly happened?" Benny said to Annie. "I've heard bits and pieces."

Annie told the story of Flanagan and the children's ball while he lay quietly on the floor beside her, watching their faces intently. Robert sat on a stool eating cookies, and Benny and Annie's mother sipped their coffee. They had to speak loudly when the lawn mower came near the house.

"Oh, nobody's going to make any big deal about a dog grabbing a kid's ball," Malcolm said. He opened the closet door to get his basketball. "What's this?" He held up Flanagan's bright ball.

Flanagan gave a happy yip and leaped for it. Annie, who had been sitting on the floor beside him, nearly fell over backward, and Robert's stool almost tipped over. Benny spilled his coffee.

"Put that ball back!" Annie's mother cried, but it was too late. Flanagan knocked it out of Malcolm's hands and with a forward thrust of his head sent it spinning toward Annie.

"Outside!" her mother said. "Out!"

Her last word rang out in sudden silence.

"Father has finished mowing," Robert said.

Annie steered Flanagan and the ball outside, and for the next half hour she played ball with him in his run. Finally, exhausted, she said, "I've had it. You play by yourself. For your first day, Flanagan, it's been busy."

She left him happily poking the ball around with his nose. As she came across the newly mowed lawn, a police car drove into the yard. *The* police car, the only one in town.

"Hi there, Annie," Chief Porter said. "You're just the one I want to see."

chapter 9

"Hello, Mr. Porter," Annie said, trying to keep her voice steady.

He was a big man, and it took him a minute to get himself out from behind the steering wheel, although Annie knew he could move very fast when he had to.

"I heard you got a new dog."

"Yes, I have. Mrs. Meyers gave him to me."

"I see." He shoved his police cap onto the back of his head and mopped his face with a big handkerchief. "Hot, isn't it?"

"Yes. Very hot." She was so tense, her leg muscles ached.

"How come Mrs. Meyers is giving away dogs? I thought they were pretty expensive animals." He was walking toward Flanagan's run.

Annie wished her father would show up, but he had put away the lawn mower and gone in through the patio doors. By now he was probably in the shower.

"They are expensive, but this one has something a little bit wrong with his knees, so he can't be a show dog. She couldn't breed him, either, in case his pups had the same fault, so she wanted to give him to someone who would love him." Annie felt as if she was chattering. She made herself stop.

"Ayuh," Chief Porter said. "I see. That makes sense. I didn't figure Emma Meyers was going to give away a good dog out of the kindness of her heart. I thought maybe the dog had a mean streak."

"Oh, *no*!" Annie was so shocked she forgot to be scared. "Flanagan is the best-natured dog you ever saw."

"Young Mrs. Hanson seemed to think he attacked her kids. Knocked one over, she said. Bruised her up some."

"He was only playing. They had a ball, and he loves to play ball." They had reached the run, and Flanagan had galloped up to the gate to greet them. "That little kid is hardly old enough to stand up, anyway. I don't think she could have had any bruises. Did you see them?"

Chief Porter smiled but didn't answer. He unlatched the gate, and Flanagan came up to him, wagging his tail. Annie prayed he wouldn't put his paws on the chief's shoulders.

"Boy, you are a big son of a gun, aren't you." Chief Porter patted Flanagan's head, and Flanagan gave his hand a big, slurpy wipe of his tongue. The chief laughed and wiped his hand on his handkerchief.

"Sit, Flanagan," Annie said, and held her breath. But Flanagan obediently sat, his head cocked on one side, looking at her. "Stay," she said. And he sat still. She could have hugged him.

"Looks like he's trained pretty good." Chief Porter looked up and said, "Hiya, Father Ben."

Annie hadn't seen Ben coming. She was relieved. He and the chief were friends. They often worked together, especially with kids in trouble.

"How you doing, Chief? Come to pay a social call? Or has Jack Anderson been at it again?"

The chief laughed. "As a matter of fact, he did say something about a barking dog keeping him awake."

"Only a tornado would keep Jack awake past nine o'clock. You know that."

"I know. I just thought I'd drop by and take a look at the monster that nearly wiped out a group of small, defenseless children." He winked at Annie.

Flanagan was quivering with his effort to sit still. "Here, boy," Annie said, and he leaped toward her. "Easy, now. Heel."

"The Bethel boy told me the dog didn't do a thing but act like a dog, and I guess I can't fault him for that. I'll tell you what, Annie. Why don't you keep him away from downtown till he's a little older. I know you got to exercise him, but take him out to the arboretum or someplace like that, where nobody hardly ever goes. We had a couple transients there last year, but that's the exception."

"Speaking of transients," Benny said, "when I showed

up for Vespers this week, there was this woman sitting way in the back. She left before I got a chance to talk to her. I suppose the church looked like a place to rest, and the service took her by surprise."

"Patty Miller told me she saw some strange woman in the alley back of her house," the chief said. "When she went out to speak to her, the woman took off. I'll keep an eye out for her."

"Vespers is candlelight," Benny said, "so I didn't get a good look at her, but she was wearing what looked like a man's overcoat that came down almost to her ankles. She was little and kind of disheveled. Before the people got there for the service, I heard her praying out loud, kind of having a one-way conversation with God, I guess. I was sorry she got away. She may need help."

"If she's still around, we'll find her." The chief turned toward his car. "That's a nice dog, Annie. Just keep him out of trouble."

"I will, really. Thanks for not arresting me."

He laughed. "See you around, fellas."

"See ya, Bernie," Benny said.

"Keep 'em virtuous." The chief hefted himself around to see out the rear window and backed quickly out of the yard.

"Whew!" Annie said. "I was worried."

"Bernie's reasonable," Benny said. "But if complaints pile up, he'll have to do something, so take care."

"Don't worry, I will."

Benny left, and Annie went inside, nervous about what her father might say if he knew that the chief of police had come on a complaint about Flanagan. He might make her give Flanagan back. But she found her parents in the kitchen drinking coffee, her father showered and cooled off except for the pinkness of sunburn on his face. He looked calm. Either her mother hadn't told him about the problem with Flanagan, or she had told him and persuaded him not to worry about it.

They both looked up when she came into the kitchen, and her mother smiled. Her father didn't smile, but he was not a big smiler at any time except when he needed to persuade his parishioners to do what he wanted them to do, like increasing their contributions.

Annie went up to her room. Malcolm's rock music was playing, and through Robert's open door she saw him reading, lying on his back on his bed with his legs hung over the headboard. No wonder he had to wear glasses.

She went into her room and flung herself on the bed. Having Flanagan certainly made life more eventful. She wondered what would happen next. Just so Father didn't make her give him back.

chapter 10

Annie woke early the next morning. She had waked up half a dozen times during the night, listening for Flanagan, but he had not barked at all, as far as she knew. Benny had calmed Father down when he found out about Chief Porter's visit. She had had a lecture from Father about keeping Flanagan away from children and what he called "populated places." He didn't want any more trouble.

She got up quietly, showered and dressed, and fixed herself a bowl of cereal and a glass of milk. No one else was up yet, although probably Robert was awake. Robert seemed always to be awake.

She made some peanut-butter-and-raspberry-jam sandwiches, packed them in her book bag with a banana, an apple, and a handful of Doggie Bones, which were not real bones. Her mother said, "God knows what they're made of, but we'll have to trust it isn't lethal." Flanagan had gobbled them down with a good deal of enthusiasm and showed no ill effects.

She let herself out the back door quietly, taking the book bag and the leash, then, at the last minute, went back to get a small carton of orange juice. She knew she'd get thirsty.

Flanagan leaped up and down with joy when he saw her coming, but although he made sounds in his throat, he didn't bark.

"We're going to the arboretum," she told him. "You'll like it. And hardly anybody ever goes there because the paths are so overgrown, it's hard to walk. I think the state foresters leave it that way on purpose so people won't hang out in there and mess it up."

They set out in the opposite direction from the one that led downtown. On this side of town the houses were spaced much farther apart and back from the street. The only person she saw was Mrs. Ainsley, the woman who made Father's horseradish. She was weeding her garden, and she looked up and waved.

Annie was walking fast, and Flanagan trotted along beside her, looking up at her every now and then, and only once in a while making a dive after a grasshopper or a quickly disappearing cat. "You're doing much better," Annie told him. "You're going to be a model dog in no time at all." She liked the way he watched her when she spoke to him, as if he were really listening to what she said and trying to understand it. Irish wolfhounds were obviously very smart.

When they got to the town limits, she told him the arboretum was about a mile farther. "It was left to the state by a man who was a botanist and very rich. He bought this huge wooded area, and he planted a lot of rare trees and flowers. Once in a while you come across a deer. They're really tame, but you mustn't chase them."

They passed a farm, where a man she didn't know was setting out vegetables for sale on a long table near the street.

"Nice day," he said.

"Beautiful," she said.

"That's a big dog you got there. Nice-looking fella. What kind is he?"

"Irish wolfhound," she said.

"Does he bite?"

"Oh, no."

He came close enough to hand her a pear from one of his trays, careful not to get too close to Flanagan. "Have a pear. Just picked."

"Thank you. That's very nice. It looks good."

"Tell your mother about us. We're new in town. Sanders is the name."

Annie told him her name, thanked him again, and moved on. She had had an uneasy feeling that one of Flanagan's joyous moods might overcome him, and he'd knock over the farmer's carefully laid-out table. Not on purpose, of course.

"The Ryans used to live there," she told Flanagan.

"They had a girl my age, but she went to the Westfield school."

She thought about school. Madison and Westfield shared Regional High School, where she would be a freshman in the fall. Making the move from the school she had gone to for so many years to the big high school scared her. She would have her own friends and classmates, but there would be hordes of kids she didn't know.

"I wish I could take you to school with me," she told Flanagan.

He looked at her and then made a dive for a squirrel who had scampered past them on top of the stone wall. "Wait till we get to the arboretum," she said. "Then you can run free."

She slowed down as they turned into the dirt road that wound around the paddock and stables of one of the few big estates left in the county. Flanagan's attention was caught by the saddle horses in the paddock.

"Do they remind you of home?" She knew Mrs. Meyers had horses.

They crossed a narrow wooden bridge and came to the entrance to the arboretum, where a small brass plaque said HANFORD STATE PARK. NO CAMPING.

She picked her way along the tangled path, letting Flanagan off the leash.

Flanagan nosed into the thick brush, smelling everything.

"I almost stepped on a porcupine here once," she told him. "You wouldn't like that. And once I saw a weasel that looked like a mink collar from somebody's coat."

Flanagan was jumping over fallen logs, digging here

and there. Once he took off after a rabbit, but she called him back and he came. She didn't want him to get too far out of sight, because there were so many paths and animal trails, she might lose him.

For a long time they rambled here and there in the woods. After a while the slight breeze died down, and gnats and mosquitoes became a nuisance. She had to call Flanagan several times to get him to follow her along another path that led out of the woods on the far side by the river. That would be a good place to have lunch and cool off.

When Flanagan saw the river, he bolted in and swam halfway across, then came back and shook himself violently, spraying her with water.

Annie waded into the river, leaving her sneakers on because of the stones. She kept going till the water reached the bottom of her shorts, then splashed her face and arms, wishing she could strip and swim. But as sure as she did, somebody would come around the bend in a canoe, probably a parishioner. She giggled at the idea of surfacing naked alongside a boat with some of the guild members in it.

She sat on the bank to dry off and eat lunch.

"We'll go back the long way around," she said. As they started off, she pointed out an aluminum building. "That's where they keep the tools they use to clean up the woods. There's an old hut built into the side of a hill, but they don't use that anymore. It's cool and dark as a dungeon in there."

Flanagan put his paws on the trunk of a tree, looking up at a small yellow bird swinging on a branch.

"A goldfinch, I think," she told him. "And look how the bark is chewed on the trunk. Porcupines do that."

A salt-smelling breeze from the ocean had started, driving away the annoying bugs and cooling everything. Annie found three lady slippers in a swampy place, looking like orchids. She wished she could take one to her mother, but it was against the law to pick them.

They wandered farther and farther into the woods. "There's the path that dead-ends at the old toolshed," she said.

Flanagan immediately started down the path, and she grabbed his collar. "No, don't go down that path. It's dark and spooky, and it just dead-ends at the hut." She had almost stepped on a snake the last time she had gone down there. It was a harmless garter snake, but it was unusually long, and it had darted almost under her feet and scared her. At camp they got points for their nature team if they held a garter snake by its tail for one minute, but she had never had the nerve to do it.

"Come *on*," she said, tugging at Flanagan's collar. "There's nothing interesting down there." She swatted at a mosquito that buzzed around her ear. "Maybe it's time to go home. I'm hot and thirsty."

She tried to turn Flanagan into the path ahead of them, but he seemed determined to go down the path to the hut. "Look," she said. "Somebody else has been wandering around here." She stooped and picked up half a wrapper from a Hershey bar. "Litterer." She put it in her pocket.

As she straightened up, Flanagan lunged, pulled loose from her hand, and raced down the path to the hut. "Oh, *Flanagan*! Come back here."

But whatever interested him was stronger than his

impulse to obey. In a moment he had disappeared. It was probably a rabbit, she thought. The one he had chased before lunch had dived into the bushes and sat still, nose quivering, thinking, as rabbits seemed to do, that if he sat still, no one could see him. Flanagan had bounded up to him and then stood sniffing at him and looking back at Annie as if to say, "What do I do now?" Then he had lost interest. Rabbits and chipmunks and squirrels were only fun if they ran.

She waited a minute, calling Flanagan. When he didn't come, she sighed and started down the path after him, stepping carefully and keeping a lookout for snakes. The trees bordering the narrow path were especially dense, making it hard to see clearly.

She heard Flanagan bark. "Silly dog," she said aloud. "Putting the fear of God into some terrified rabbit." She readjusted her book bag on her back. It was hot. The fresh breeze didn't reach through this part of the woods. She was getting annoyed with Flanagan. He would simply have to learn to obey.

He barked again as she came to the end of the path and found him facing the low door of the shed built into a rise in the land.

"There's nothing in there, silly," she said, "unless it's spiders and creepy crawlies. What's a big, noble dog like you barking at spiders for?"

He ran to her side, but before she could grab him, he trotted back again to the door and barked.

"You're hopeless." She went up to him, took the leash out, and snapped it onto his collar. But even with the leash, she had trouble making him go with her.

"Flanagan! Heel!"

As she spoke, she heard a sudden creaking sound and turned toward the door of the hut. She stood stock-still as the door slowly opened. All she could see was a dim face with burning eyes and a pair of pale hands holding a pistol aimed at her head.

chapter 11

When she could speak, she said in a faint voice, "Please, I'm sorry. We didn't know there was anyone in there."

"You knew all right, Valenti." The woman's voice was cracked. "You won't give me a minute's peace. I know you, Valenti." The gun wavered, pointing at Flanagan and then back at Annie. The hut was so dark, she could not make out the woman's face at all.

"I'm not Valenti," Annie said. "I'm Annie MacDougal. We were just out for a walk."

"Don't give me that malarkey. You've always been out to get me. I'm on to you."

"I could show you my ID bracelet," Annie said, desperately trying to think of something to convince this woman. "It has my name on it."

The woman hesitated. "Throw it over here. But easy, or I'll blow your head off."

Annie fumbled with the catch on the ID bracelet, at the same time trying to hold Flanagan still. He was longing to investigate this stranger and her hut. With her free hand Annie tossed the bracelet toward the woman's hand, but it fell at her feet.

"Good aim." The woman gave a sudden wild cackle of laughter. "Maybe you aren't Valenti. She couldn't hit the side of a barn door." Without taking her eyes off Annie, she stooped and picked up the bracelet. Quickly she glanced at it. "Too dark to see, but I don't see any capital *V*. Got a little *v*, though."

"No, there aren't any *v*'s." Slowly Annie spelled out her name: Anne Adair MacDougal.

The woman held it up high for a better look. "Maybe you stole it."

"Of course I didn't." Annie was beginning to feel more angry than frightened. If it weren't for the gun, she'd have just walked off. She said, "What's *your* name?"

"Cora," the woman said absentmindedly, still examining the bracelet. Then she glared at Annie. "Oh, no you don't. You're trying to trap me. Even if you aren't Valenti, she sent you. You're going to turn me in."

"Lady," Annie said, "I don't know Valenti, and I'm not going to tell anybody I even saw you, if that's what you want. It's none of my business who you are."

"Then why'd you ask?"

"I was just being polite."

In a softer, almost wistful voice, the woman said, "I was polite once. I was well brought up. Brushed my teeth twice a day, bath every night."

Annie suddenly felt sorry for her. "Look, do you need help? Can I do anything for you?"

On guard again, Cora said, "I don't need any help. I'm doing fine. Why've you got that pony with you?"

"He's not a pony. He's a dog."

"Now I *know* you're lying."

"He's an Irish wolfhound. They're very big dogs."

"If they're all like him, they're dinosaurs. If I let you go, you got to promise not to tell where I am."

"I promise." The gun was aimed at her chest now. "Really, I won't mention it."

"Swear it?"

"I swear."

"Say 'I swear it by Jesus Christ, the Virgin Mary, and the Holy Spirit.' "

Annie repeated what she had said.

"All right. You can go." The woman tossed the gun behind her into the hut. Annie held her breath waiting for it to go off, but there was only a faint thud.

"Good-bye," Annie said. "I won't forget my promise."

As she and Flanagan turned back up the path, Flanagan resisting all the way, the woman stayed where she was, watching them. Annie glanced back quickly as they took the turn onto the other trail, but the door was lost in the shrubbery.

Even so, Cora's loud cackle of laughter followed Annie, and words that sounded like "water pistol," but she was in too much of a hurry to pay attention. Holding Flanagan close to her on the leash, she tried to run on the uneven, overgrown path, bumping into Flanagan every few minutes. He whimpered, wanting to be free of the leash.

"If I let you go, you'll go right back there." Annie's breath came in short gasps, as if she had been running a long way. Perspiration dripped into her eyes, and her chest hurt. Now that they were some distance away from that scary woman, she was more frightened than she had been when she faced her. Glancing back often to make sure she wasn't being followed, she took the wrong path twice and had to turn back. There seemed to be no end to the woods.

Finally she stumbled past the sign that said HANFORD STATE PARK. A smaller wooden sign that she had probably seen before without noticing it lay in the bushes. It said NO CAMPING, NO FIRES, NO PICKING OF FLOWERS OR CUTTING OF TREES. It looked as if it had lain there a long time, half hidden by weeds and fallen leaves.

Annie took a long breath of relief when they reached the road that ran past the horse farm. She let Flanagan wallow in the shallow brook that ran along the side of the road. The water she scooped up in her hands and splashed on her face felt cold and good, waking her out of what had seemed like a nightmare.

"I'm overreacting," she said to Flanagan. "It was just some eccentric lady going through town, one of those people Benny says don't have a place to live. It's a hot day, and she lucked out, finding a cool place to rest. I scared her. Probably cops and other people make her move along all the time. We just hardly ever see vagrants in this town."

She watched a boy take his horse over one of the jumps in the field, clearing it beautifully. She wished she knew how to ride like that. Coming back, he saw her and waved. It was one of the Sheaffer boys, whose family owned the estate. They went to Phillips Andover.

"Valenti," Annie said aloud as she walked along the road. "I wonder who Valenti is, and why she thought I was Valenti."

When she got home, she put Flanagan in his run and filled his water dish from the hose. "You got enough exercise for a while."

Her mother and Robert were in the kitchen. Her mother was studying a pair of unpainted wooden bookends, and Robert was talking about the hopeless Daniels kids.

"The kid sister," he said, "must be lined with lead. I turn her on her back, show her how to tip her head back, chest up, and does she float? She sinks like a two-ton truck."

"Don't embellish, dear," his mother said.

"Ruthie's swan dive would send any self-respecting swan to a psychiatrist."

"If I could learn to carve instead of buying these things from George," Annie's mother said, picking up a bookend, "I could get them the shape I want. Maybe I'll take a woodcarving course this winter."

Annie poured herself a glass of water. She longed to tell them about the strange woman in the arboretum, but she had promised.

"When Ruthie dives, she goes in like an elephant landing flat on his belly."

"Stomach," his mother said absently, turning the bookend this way and that.

"People don't do stomach flops, Mom. They do belly flops."

Annie opened the *Weekly Chronicle* and fanned herself with it. Her mother loved to read the "Town Chat" column because it was full of non sequiturs. A few weeks ago an item had said, "Ella Fleming was walking across the square at lunchtime yesterday when someone in a blue Chevrolet blew his horn. It turned out to be a friend of hers." Her mother had thought it was very funny. Annie didn't think it was all that hilarious, but maybe it was.

"Have a nice time with Flanagan?" her mother asked.

Annie said yes and told her about Mr. Sanders's fruit-and-vegetable stand. She opened up the paper, looked at the front page, and gasped.

"What heart-stopping news do they have this week?" her mother said. "Has Ella Fleming been crossing the square again?"

"Look," Annie said faintly. She spread out the paper.

Robert and their mother looked over her shoulder. There was a blurred picture of Flanagan in his run with a caption that read: PET OR MONSTER? The headline on the story read: MONSTER DOG SCARES COMMUNITY.

"Oh, no!" her mother said. "Who got that picture?"

"Jack Anderson, you can bet," Robert said, "with his superexpensive camera that he doesn't know how to use. What else does it say?" He read the story aloud. " 'Father MacDougal's daughter Annie has a new pet that is causing quite a stir. It's one of the Irish wolfhounds from the Meyers kennel (And some people are asking why Emma Meyers gave away one of her valuable pups. Tricky disposition, maybe?). Already the dog has caused a good deal of trouble. Night-long barking disturbs the neighbors. Small children have been bowled over and narrowly escaped injury. One of the mothers, who wished not to give her name, has complained to the police. Chief Porter has the matter under investigation. Too bad, Annie MacDougal. Next time get a Chihuahua.' "

Annie was so shocked she could hardly breathe. She looked at her mother, who was standing tight-lipped and arms folded.

"It's those stinking Andersons," Robert said. "I'm going to give him a piece of my mind."

His mother grabbed him by the collar. "You stay right where you are."

"But, Mom, it's a pack of lies. We can't take it lying down."

"I have to think," his mother said.

Someone ran up the back steps, and Malcolm burst into the kitchen swinging his tennis racket. "Hey, I'm in the *Chronicle*. Did you see it? Page five." He grabbed the paper and turned to the page. " 'Malcolm MacDougal, county singles champion for the past two years, will have a rematch with Edward "Ned" Dumas, who barely beat him out this year. The two will face off in the YMCA tournament, the week of August 29.' " He looked up, his face glowing. "How about that? A little PR never hurt, huh? I'm going to massa-cree that Dumas kid, and they'll probably put my picture . . ." He stopped. "What's the matter with you guys?"

Silently Robert handed him the front page.

"What is it? What . . . oh, no!" He read the story, moving his lips as if he were back in the second grade, Annie thought. She was angry with him because he was on page five, and he was happy. She was on page one, and her life was in ashes.

They all heard the motorcycle roar into the backyard, but nobody reacted. Benny bounded up the steps and into the kitchen. "Greetings, gang," he said. "What's the good word?" Then, as Malcolm's had, his face changed. "What's wrong?"

Malcolm handed him the paper. For a second Annie thought, remorsefully, I've spoiled Malcolm's big moment. But then she forgot everything but Flanagan. She would surely lose him now.

Benny's face darkened. "Well, what are you all standing around here for? Get your helmet, Annie. We've got people to talk to."

"You'd better wait for Dougal . . . ," her mother began.

"Not this time," Benny said. "Dougal doesn't know how to deal with dirty business. I do." He grabbed Annie's arm. "Come on, we've got people to see."

She was still strapping on her helmet with one hand and hanging on to Benny with the other as the motorcycle roared out of the yard.

chapter 12

They began with the newspaper. Feeling conspicuous, Annie tagged along behind Benny as he strode through the newsroom, where three people were working at computers. He brushed off offers of help.

"No, thanks," he said, swinging his helmet in his hand. "I want to see the boss."

The editor, a young man named Endicott, had recently taken over the editorship when the former man retired. He was from out of town, and Annie knew him by sight but had never talked to him.

He looked up, startled, as Benny knocked on the open

door and walked in without waiting to be asked. "Good day, Father," Endicott said. "Can I help you?"

"I hope so." Benny was not smiling. He pulled the front page from his pocket and laid it on the desk facing the editor. "This is Father MacDougal's daughter, the person who is the subject of this scurrilous story on your front page."

"Scurrilous?" Mr. Endicott was trying to smile, but Annie noticed he pushed his chair back from his desk, distancing himself from Benny. "Always watch the body language," Benny had told her once. Mr. Endicott's body language suggested alarm. "*Scurrilous* is a strong word," he said.

"Yes, it is." Benny smiled for the first time, but it was not a friendly smile. "Frankly, Mr. Endicott, it's a pack of lies."

Endicott tried hard to bristle. "I don't want to contradict you, Father. . . ."

"Then don't," Benny said.

"But my reporters are usually quite accurate."

"Usually, yes. Not this time. Tell him, Annie."

Annie hadn't expected that. She took a deep breath, glanced sideways at Benny, and said, "Well, first of all, there is nothing wrong with Mrs. Meyers's dog . . . my dog . . . except a fault in his hocks."

"Hocks?" Endicott gave her the kind of smarmy smile she had always hated in adults who talked down to kids. "I'm not a dog man, myself."

"Knees," Annie said. She was beginning to forget her self-consciousness. This man was a twerp. "His knees don't conform to AKC standards. American Kennel Club."

"I see," Endicott said vaguely. "I guess they're pretty fussy."

"That is why she gave him to me, to give him a good home. *Not* because there is anything wrong with his disposition. He has a very gentle disposition. He just happens to be big. He does not bark at night. Except the first night, for about ten minutes. He does not intentionally knock over small children. He was trying to play ball with them. I have a witness. Todd Bethel . . ."

"Yes," Mr. Endicott said dryly, "I have already had a call from Todd Bethel."

Annie felt the first warm glow she'd had in some time. "Mrs. Hanson was upset because her little kid fell down, and she thought Flanagan . . . my dog . . . pushed her, but he didn't. She complained to Chief Porter, and he came to see me. He was satisfied with my explanation. There is no investigation going on that I know of. You can ask him. . . ."

"You should have asked him," Benny said. "Don't reporters normally check out a story?"

"Certainly." Mr. Endicott was fiddling with his glasses frames. He laid them carefully on the desk.

"And I don't want a Chihuahua." Annie moved back. Watch your own body language, she thought, but she suddenly felt amazed and a little alarmed at her own flow of words. She had probably sounded like a sassy brat. But Benny gave her a quick smile.

"So of course," Benny said, "you'll want to print a retraction. On the front page. Nasty rumors can get started in a town the size of this." His voice was milder now, almost fatherly, although Mr. Endicott was probably ten years older than he was. It was the pastoral voice; Annie heard it often when her father dispensed advice, but Benny didn't often use it. "We wouldn't want Mrs. Hanson to be encouraged to start a lawsuit that she could only lose. And it would be a pity to make a pariah of a fine dog like Ian Flanagan of Wild Rose Farm. I'm sure Mrs. Meyers, for one, would not be happy about that."

"Of course," Mr. Endicott muttered.

"You don't want to take just my word for it, naturally. Why don't you give Chief Porter a call while we're here? We may as well get this thing straightened out." Benny's voice now was almost friendly, as if he and Endicott were both seekers of the truth.

Endicott hesitated a moment, but then he reached for the phone.

"Four-zero-six, two-two-nine-one," Benny said helpfully.

Endicott dialed. He arranged his face and spoke in a hearty, friendly voice, one public personage to another. "Good afternoon, Chief Porter. This is Harold Endicott at the *Chronicle*."

Annie could hear the chief's deep voice, but not what he said. Endicott's expression changed, the confidence fading.

"Yes," he said, "it was an unfortunate slip."

The sound of the chief's voice rumbled again. Benny gave Annie a quick wink.

"It certainly should have been checked with you. Yes, Chief, I agree. We'll be more careful about that in future. Thank you for your cooperation, sir." He hung up. His face was red. He scribbled something on a pad, and not looking up, he said, "There's no investigation."

"And of course you will want to print that retraction."

"Naturally," Endicott snapped.

"Thank you." Benny thrust out his hand, and Mr. Endicott had no choice but to shake it. "I know you're new in town, and we wish you the best of luck. Small towns take a while to psych out. I know—I'm from the city myself."

Endicott nodded and muttered something that Annie didn't hear. He half rose from his desk as a reluctant gesture of courtesy.

"Thank you," Annie said, but he was already on the phone, a different phone, angrily summoning a reporter named Al Davis.

"Davis will take the heat," Benny said as they left the building. "He's used to it."

"Where are we going now?" she said.

"A chat with Mrs. Hanson."

When Mrs. Hanson saw Annie, she frowned. She was on her front porch, her youngest child in her lap. "Have you got rid of that dog?" she said.

"No," Annie said. "That's what we wanted to talk to you about. Do you know Father Ben Vitale?"

She nodded and held her child closer, as if she thought something might happen to him in such dangerous company.

"We were upset by that story in the paper," Benny said.

"I'll bet you were," Mrs. Hanson said.

Ben sat on the rail of her porch, swinging his legs. She scowled at him and pushed her chair back, just as Mr. Endicott had.

Benny looked at her thoughtfully for a second. "That's a cute youngster. What's his name?"

Mrs. Hansen looked at him suspiciously. "Rudy," she said.

"Was it Rudy who fell down when Annie's dog jumped for the ball?"

"No. It was Evelyn Rae. What of it?"

"Oh, nothing at all," Benny said. "I was just thinking that with such cute kids, it's no wonder you're a little overprotective."

Her voice rose. "I'm not *over*protective. That monster of a dog knocked Evelyn Rae flat. She could have cracked her skull."

"How lucky she didn't. But Todd Bethel agrees with Annie that it was an accident. And Todd has no ax to grind. Perhaps your concern for your children, your natural concern, made you . . ."

She interrupted him. "Look, I don't belong to your church, and I don't have to listen to your lectures. I saw what I saw."

Benny nodded gravely. Then he said, "Annie, leave us alone for a minute, would you please?"

Annie went back to the sidewalk and leaned against the motorcycle, willing herself not to look toward the house. She was dying to know what Ben was saying. The worst of it was, he would probably never tell her. He was like her father; he put a high value on confidentiality. Priests were as bad as psychiatrists that way.

The conversation seemed to go on and on. Annie got more and more impatient. Finally she heard Benny say, "Have a good day, Mrs. Hanson." That was something he never said; he made fun of it for being a meaningless cliché.

He came down the walk and straddled the motorcycle. "Get aboard," he said, revving the engine.

When he let her off at her house, she said, "What were you talking about?"

"Dogs," he said. He pushed back his helmet and grinned at her. "My success with Mrs. Hanson, on a scale of one to ten, was roughly eight and a half. She won't bring suit because she knows she'd lose. But she won't keep her mouth shut, either."

She saw that that was all she would get out of him.

"Remind Robert that he said he'd go to the retarded kids' concert tonight. Don't let him forget his harmonica. I'll pick him up around seven." And he was gone before she could even say thank you.

Her father came out of his study as she started upstairs. "I don't think much of that story in the *Chronicle*," he said.

"None of us do, Father." Annie felt exhausted. She wanted to lie down. "There's going to be a front-page retraction."

"Indeed?" He studied her face.

If he says I have to get rid of Flanagan, she thought, I'll leave home. I'll take Flanagan and hitch a ride somewhere. I'll say I'm sixteen and I'll get a job washing dishes or something.

"Benny?" her father said.

"Benny and I," she said. She sounded more defiant than she meant to.

Surprisingly, he smiled. "Being a friend isn't easy," he said, and went back into his study.

She didn't know whether he meant it wasn't easy for Benny to be her friend, or for her to be Flanagan's friend, but at least he hadn't said she couldn't keep her dog.

chapter 13

Annie was ironing shirts for her father. She was the only one patient enough to do them the way he liked them. Flanagan, who was allowed in the kitchen now if Annie's mother wasn't cooking, lay on a patch of sunshine with his head on his paws, watching her.

"I'm ironing Father's shirts," she said. "It's one of my few talents."

Her parents were going to Sherry's camp in southern New Hampshire for three days to see Sherry dance in the final concert and to bring her home. Annie had mixed feelings about Sherry's return. She missed her, but she liked having their bedroom to herself. Sherry took up a lot of space wherever she was. After some debate her mother had agreed that Annie and the boys could take care of themselves without a sitter.

"Sherry will love you," Annie told Flanagan. "Last year she had a kitten, but she forgot about it one night and it got run over."

Flanagan got up and wandered around the kitchen, poking at cupboard doors and lifting his head to sniff at countertops.

"Tomorrow we'll go out to the arboretum." She had avoided going there since they had encountered the woman, but her conscience bothered her. If she couldn't tell anyone about her, at least she should make sure the woman was all right.

After she had seen the woman, she had read an article in her father's copy of *Time* or *Newsweek* about people being turned out of mental institutions and left to cope on their own. She'd asked Benny about it. He had strong opinions; he had often seen people roaming around Boston, on the Common or in the back streets, who were homeless and not mentally able to handle it. During that conversation she had almost told him about the woman in the toolshed, but a promise was a promise.

Her mother came in carrying a big bag of fresh vegetables from Mr. Sanders's roadside stand: lettuce, English peas, tomatoes.

"Cook the peas tonight while they're fresh," she told Annie.

"Benny's bringing pizzas."

"All the more reason to have some real food."

Robert came in trying to finish an ice-cream bar without getting the chocolate on his shirt.

"Robert," his mother said, "are those my old combat boots?"

"Yeah. I found them in the attic. You had big feet, Mother."

"I still have."

"Why are you wearing them?" Annie said. They were much too big for him.

"I wanted to see how it felt to be a hippie."

"You have to have long hair," Annie said, "and a dirty T-shirt and sing Dylan songs and march on Washington."

"Oh, dear." Her mother laughed. She unloaded a big box of blueberries from the paper bag and offered one to the inquisitive Flanagan, who sniffed it and dropped it on the floor.

Robert went out to the mailbox as the mailman drove away. It took him awhile to come back. When he did, he had an amazed look on his face. "Guess what?" His voice rose. "Mom, look!" He was waving a letter.

"What is it?"

"You know that story I sent to *Scholastic*?"

"What about it?" Annie sensed his excitement.

"I won a prize! Fifty bucks!" He held up the check. "And they're going to publish it. *Wow!*" He ran across the kitchen, tripping over the loose toes of the combat boots. He stumbled and fell and lay on his back, still waving the check and the letter. "I'm a published author!"

"Robert!" Annie tried to hug him. One of his boots fell off.

"Rob, that's wonderful!" His mother hugged Flanagan. "Flanagan, Robert is an author!"

Annie's father and Mr. Thompson appeared in the doorway, looking puzzled.

"Has someone won the state lottery?" Annie's father said.

Flanagan, recognizing an old friend, bounded up to Mr. Thompson.

"Robert sold a story to *Scholastic*," Annie said. "Fifty dollars! Hi, Mr. Thompson. How are you?" She had been hoping that Mrs. Meyers would not have seen the *Chronicle* story about Flanagan.

"Fine and dandy. I just got back from Boothbay. Congratulations, young man."

Robert struggled to his feet. "Thank you. Please excuse the boots. And the hysteria." He looked at his father.

"I am impressed," his father said. He shook Robert's hand.

"It's nice to see you, Mr. Thompson," Annie's mother said. "Would you like some coffee? Tea?"

"No, I thank you. I wanted to tell you I just caught up with that scandalous story in the paper. I gave the editor a piece of my mind."

"There's going to be a retraction," Annie said. "Flanagan didn't do anything bad at all."

"I know that." Mr. Thompson rubbed Flanagan's head. "I know him. Well, I'll just be going. I'll be expecting to see your work on the telly soon, young man."

As soon as Mr. Thompson had gone, Annie's father said, "We should be on our way. Are we packed?"

"Ready to roll," his wife said. "Annie, you have the phone number at the inn, if you need us."

"We'll be fine," Annie said. "Can Flanagan sleep in my room while you're gone?"

"I don't think we'd better start that. He can stay in

till bedtime." She patted Flanagan. "Take good care of them, boy."

Fifteen minutes later Annie and Robert watched their parents drive off in their mother's car.

"Good thing she's driving," Robert said. "At Father's rate of speed, they wouldn't make it till next week."

Annie cooked the peas and washed the blueberries and set the table in the kitchen so that Flanagan could be with them without breaking any rules.

Malcolm was playing Paul Simon's *Graceland* several decibels higher than he dared do when his parents were home. Robert had gone to the store to buy ice cream to celebrate his new status as professional writer. He was also going to buy some overseas postage stamps for what he called his career as a Freedom Writer. He wrote many letters to heads of state who held political prisoners, asking them to free the prisoners: "Dear Prime Minister," "Dear General," "Dear Secretary/President." He showed them to Annie to correct his spelling.

Robert was the one Annie had considered telling about the woman in the arboretum. Robert was so much like a part of her own self, it didn't seem so bad to tell him. But so far, she had not.

"Tomorrow," she said to Flanagan, "we will definitely go see if she's still there."

Robert with the ice cream and Benny with a stack of pizzas arrived almost at the same time. Malcolm was downstairs in a flash, bursting with anticipation.

"I smell pizza," he said. "No anchovies, I hope." He set his tape player on the counter.

"Anchovies, I hope," Annie said.

"Both. All kinds." Benny deposited the stack of good-smelling boxes on the table and grabbed Robert's hand. "When are they giving you the Pulitzer?"

"Next year." Robert was grinning broadly.

"Flanagan, get away from the pizzas," Malcolm said. "Let's eat."

"I got one plain cheese for Flanagan," Benny said. "And if it sticks in his teeth, don't blame me."

When they were seated around the table, Malcolm said, "Rob, if you were a sportswriter, you could write about me."

"Only I'm not a sportswriter."

They stopped talking as Benny said grace.

"I hope the Lord could hear that," Benny said, "over your tape player. *Could* we turn it down a tad so we can converse without screaming?"

Reluctantly, Malcolm turned down the volume slightly.

They had demolished the pizzas and started on Robert's four kinds of ice cream when there was a sudden loud knocking on the back door. They all stopped talking, and Flanagan ran to the door, barking.

"Only cops knock like that," Malcolm said.

"I'll get it." Robert went to the door.

Jack Anderson stood there, even more red in the face than usual. "I might as well be living in the middle of Times Square," he shouted above the sound of the Talking Heads tape that Malcolm had switched to. "I want you to know I'm reporting this to the police. You are ruining the neighborhood." His lip trembled. He turned on his heel and marched down the steps.

Annie was the first to react. "Mr. Anderson," she called after him, but he didn't stop. "Malcolm, turn down that blasted tape. Flanagan, stop barking!"

"Take it easy," Benny said. "I'll deal with this." He went outside and followed Mr. Anderson home.

Annie felt like hitting somebody, but she wasn't sure whom. Just when her mother had decided she was old enough to handle things at home, something like this had to happen.

Robert was pale. "Someday," he said. "Someday I am going to slug that guy, old man or no old man. He's spoiled more things for more people in this town than anybody living. He's the one ought to be locked up."

"A thousand firecrackers," Malcolm said. "I'd like to plant a thousand firecrackers under his bed and set them all off at once."

Benny came back. "All I got was a door slammed in my face. I must be losing my touch."

Malcolm shut off the tape, and they ate their melting ice cream, trying unsuccessfully to recapture the fun they had been having.

"What I'm really going to do," Robert said, "is put the Andersons in a book."

"I made a cake," Annie said. "It's only a mix, but it looks okay." She got up to get it. "I made it last night, and Mr. Anderson almost made me forget it."

Flanagan's alert ears heard the car engine seconds before the rest of them did.

"Now what?" Malcolm went to look.

"Flanagan!" Annie grabbed him and held his muzzle shut to stop his barking.

"Oh, no!" Malcolm said.

"Who is it?"

"Chief Porter."

"Never mind," Benny said. "We weren't doing anything." He got up and opened the screen door. "You're just in time, Bernie. We're about to enjoy a spectacular chocolate layer cake."

Chief Porter came in, patting his protruding stomach. "Just what I need." He pulled up a chair and sat down. "Mind if I make myself at home? I just had a nasty experience."

Maybe it's not us, Annie thought. "What was it, Chief?"

"Skinheads," he said. "Half a dozen skinheads hit town on their infernal machines. . . . Ben, when you going to get a car?"

"When the parish raises my pay," Ben said.

"Skinheads," Malcolm said. "They're scary."

"What did they do?" Annie said.

"Rode around scaring folks. Left some nasty racist graffiti on the fence behind the Catholic church, had a chat with some of our locals boys. I got hold of the highway patrol, and they ran 'em out of town. Called me Fatso—how do you like that? Me with my girlish figure." He was joking, but he was plainly upset.

Annie gave him some ice cream and a piece of cake and made him fresh coffee.

"Do you think they'll come back?" Malcolm said.

"Let's hope not. But if you see 'em, give me a call right off."

"We just had one of Jack Anderson's friendly visits," Ben said. "We thought you were coming to arrest us."

"Yeah, he called up and tried to give me an earful right

after I got back. Wild party going on, he said. Parents away. I won't repeat in polite company what I told him."

Flanagan was sitting beside the chief with his head on the chief's knee. Chief Porter patted him. "Dog, I'm glad to see you know how to play up to city hall."

"I'll bet Mr. Anderson would have been a skinhead if he'd been in the right generation," Robert said. "They're all a bunch of haters."

"Well, I guess they're one of those jokes Mother Nature likes to play on us," Chief Porter said. "Like hurricanes and black flies."

"Father would say we have to rise above them," Robert said.

"Guess he's right." The chief stood up. "That was mighty fine ice cream and cake and coffee, and I don't mind telling you, I needed it."

"Chief Porter," Malcolm said seriously, "if you need a posse or anything, let us know. I got quite a gang of friends."

"I appreciate that, Malcolm. And good luck in your tennis match."

After he had gone, Annie said, "Well, at least it wasn't Flanagan."

chapter 14

Before she left with Flanagan for her walk to the arboretum the next morning, Annie made a meat loaf for dinner and got some of Mr. Sanders's new potatoes and Kentucky Wonder beans ready to cook. It was kind of fun being in charge.

"Today," she told Flanagan, "we're going to see about that woman. She's probably been gone a long time, but we'll find out. If she's still there, maybe I can talk to Benny about places where people like that can go, without actually telling him about her." She felt guilty about not having gone before, but still she was not eager to go. Maybe they'd get a gun waved in their faces again, and she couldn't be absolutely sure it wasn't a real gun.

She thought of the gang of skinheads and shivered thinking of what they might do to a woman like that if they found her.

"When I start school, we're going to have to work out a different system," she told him. "We'll walk in the afternoon, when I get home. Maybe by that time, I can take you through town again to the meadow. It's closer. You're getting so good."

She stopped to tell Mr. Sanders how good the peas were. He introduced her to his little girl, and she told him about Sherry. "She's coming home day after tomorrow," she said to the child. "Maybe you can be friends."

The child smiled shyly and stood close to her father.

"That'd be nice," Mr. Sanders said. He gave Annie two big red plums.

It was a cool day with a light cover of gray clouds. Mr. Sanders had said as they left him, "Might rain." She hoped it wouldn't before they got home. At this time of year you could begin to feel autumn sneaking in on you. Autumn and high school. She didn't want to think about that.

They needed rain. The road sent up little clouds of dust under their feet. In the woods on their left, some bird was making a clacky metallic sound.

At the turn into the arboretum she hesitated. She would rather have gone on up the road, swinging around the arboretum to the river. The air was humid, in spite of the coolness; it had that breath-stopping oppression that comes sometimes before the rain starts. It would be worse in the woods, where not much air circulated, even on a breezy day. But she had promised herself that she would check on the woman called Cora.

"Here goes nothing," she said, heading Flanagan into the path by the sign. "It's a good thing Mr. Anderson doesn't know about Cora. He'd have Chief Porter out here arresting her for illegal camping or something. He and his wife must be very unhappy people. But it's a good thing they married each other, I guess."

Flanagan cocked his head, listening, and then dashed off after a squirrel, who let him get close before he leaped up a tree and chattered tauntingly.

"There's one kind of dog that can climb trees," Annie told him. "Basenjis. Don't you wish you could?"

She decided to go to the shed first, before they went down to the river for lunch. She wanted to get it over with before she started thinking of reasons for not going there at all.

She walked fast, pushing through the dense overgrowth, not stopping to look for flowers. She stubbed her toe on the root of a tree and almost fell. The midges swarmed around her face, one getting in her eye. She was stupid to have come in here on a day like this. It was hard to breathe.

When she came to the turnoff to the shed, she called Flanagan back and attached the leash, laughing at his look of reproach. "Well, you never know," she said.

The door to the toolshed was half open. She stopped. No one appeared. "Hello?" Her voice sounded hollow. "Mrs. Cora?" she said. The only sounds were the sounds of the woods.

"Well, let's take a look," she said to Flanagan. She

didn't want to look. She had come and the woman wasn't here. Wasn't it best to leave? But she walked slowly toward the entrance, holding Flanagan on a short leash while he strained to dash into the shed. "Stop it," she said. "Hold still."

She had to stoop to look into the shed. For a moment she couldn't see anything, but as her eyes grew used to the dimness, she said, "Look!" A worn-down broom leaned against the wall. The dirt floor had been swept, and all the trash and spiderwebs she remembered were gone. A small, rusty hibachi stood near the entrance, with a bag of charcoal briquets half gone. A board swept clean served as a shelf for two cans of condensed milk, a box of shredded wheat, two tomatoes, and a rusty can opener. In the corner an old coat was spread out for a bed.

Annie stood staring at it. Someone really was living here. If you could call it living. "Sit, Flanagan," she said impatiently as he pulled on the leash, eager to explore the shed. "This isn't your house."

She didn't know what to do. There really wasn't much here. Maybe the woman had gone, leaving what she didn't want. But if you were living in the rough, you wouldn't leave food behind, or a coat. She remembered Benny mentioning the long men's coat the woman in church had been wearing. Should she look and see if it was that kind of coat? She couldn't tell from where she stood.

"Who are you?"

She recognized the voice even before she turned around, but she also knew there was something different about it.

The woman stood in the path with her feet apart,

keeping a wary eye on Flanagan, who was now trying to bound up to her. Annie jerked on his leash, and he sat down abruptly.

"Who are you?" she said again.

She not only sounded different, she looked different. Not that Annie had seen her clearly before, but she had seen the wildness in her eyes. Now they were suspicious, but not glaring with rage. She was a short, stocky woman with a ragged haircut. Her hair was a faded reddish blond, thin and frizzled as if she had had a permanent that went wrong. But this was not a beauty-parlor kind of woman. Her clothes were shabby and faded: a dark blue cotton skirt that hung unevenly almost to her ankles, a man's blue work shirt that was too big, worn black shoes, and white ankle socks. She was carrying a bag of groceries. Annie tried to think where the nearest grocery store was. It would be the convenience store across the river, a good two miles from here.

"I'm the one who was here the other day," Annie said.

"What other day?" The woman stepped back as Flanagan again pulled toward her.

"Don't you remember? My dog came down here, and I came to get him, and you drove us away." She paused. "You said your name was Cora."

"Any fool knows that," the woman said.

Annie felt confused. "You called me Valenti."

The woman scowled, and for a moment she looked more as she had before. "You aren't Valenti. Did she send you?"

"I don't know her. I never heard of anyone by that name." Annie wished she could leave now. The woman had a shelter, she had groceries, she must have at least a little money. She didn't need Annie's help. But there was no way to get past her without asking her to move.

The woman seemed to think over what Annie had said and then to accept it. "I get paranoid, you know, when I'm off the med."

"The med?"

"The medication." She said it impatiently, as if Annie were stupid. "Thorazine."

"Oh." Annie didn't know what Thorazine was. "Are you sick?"

The woman laughed, a funny little bark of laughter that had no amusement in it. "You could say that. Why else was I shut up in Danvers for twenty-one years?"

Annie knew about the big hospital for the mentally ill in Danvers. You could see it, driving by, perched on a hill like a tremendous fortress. "But you're out now," she said, not knowing what else to say.

"They turned us out, a whole bunch of us. Deinstitutionalization." She said the word syllable by syllable, curling her lip in scorn. " 'You'll be just fine out in the real world, Cora.' " She was using a different voice, high and precise. " 'You'll adjust. Just remember to take your medication, dear. Never mind if it makes your mouth turn numb as death and your tongue feel like worms and your thoughts scramble like letters in a Scrabble game and you feel sick unto death. Never *mind* that, Cora. You can function. Mrs. Valenti has this lovely halfway house, Cora. She'll help you get used to the real world.' " She laughed that hard laugh again, and Annie heard the despair in it. She gestured to the toolshed. "Welcome to the real world."

"Did you leave the halfway house?"

"I split, dearie. I packed my ragbag and split. Who

needs it? The woman's a sadist. That's how she gets her kicks. Halfway house. Halfway to hell. Do you want some lunch?"

The abrupt change left Annie speechless for a moment. "No, thank you, I have some." She indicated the book bag slung over her shoulders. "We're going to the river for a picnic. I just stopped to see if you were all right."

The woman studied her. She had small black eyes, like raisins. "That's a switch. Not too many people ever gave a damn."

"Do you have a family?"

Cora tossed her head. "Had some once. They got sick of coming to see me. A crazy hospital isn't exactly people's favorite place to visit. My mother died. She was the only one that always came."

"Have you . . . have you got everything you need?"

"For now. I've got money enough. They paid me twelve dollars a week at the hospital, the last few years. I did work for them. I saved the money. It'll last a while."

"It's going to get too cold to stay here."

"Not for a while. I don't look all that far ahead. The Lord will provide." Again the bitter, sarcastic laugh. "You going to tell on me? They'll throw me out. 'No camping, no fires.' Well, I don't pick the flowers or chop down the trees. You going to tell?"

"No. I told you the other day I wouldn't."

"I don't remember you being here." She frowned and shook her head. "I'm not going to take the med, see. Only when I need to go get some food, and I don't want to attract attention."

Annie wondered if she didn't know how much attention she would attract even now, when she was acting relatively sane.

"So I need to be someplace like this, where I can go crazy as I want and nobody to stop me. I got two pills left. They'll tide me over for now."

"What if . . ." Annie paused, not wanting to insult her. "What if you get so sick you forget about the medicine? Something might happen to you."

"Something's already happened to me, dearie. I went crazy when I was eighteen. Just starting college. Bang. Doctors, psychiatrists, you name it. Family ran out of money. Danvers. Shock treatment. You ever have shock treatment?"

"No," Annie said faintly.

"Well, you haven't lived. Every American child should have shock treatment." She changed her tone, sounding very tired all at once. "Don't mind me. I get kind of bitter. They didn't know what they were doing. At least shocks keep the patient quiet. Who can blame them? They've got all these nuts, acting up. . . ." She shrugged. "Does that dog bite?"

"No. He's very friendly."

"I ought to get me a dog, for protection."

"You could get one at the Humane Society."

"Yeah?" For a moment she looked interested. "I don't know how to do anything. I didn't even know how to buy groceries. Had to watch other people do it first."

"I could get you a dog if you want one."

The woman sighed. "No. I'd forget to feed it. It'd die on me." She took a prescription bottle out of her pocket and held it up, unscrewing the top. "Two left. That's my med. That gets me to the grocery store and back." She shook the big tablets into her hand. "Lifeline. Death line. Depends how you look at it."

A chipmunk leaped from one branch to another, just over her head. Flanagan barked. The woman reacted with terror, jumping backward. She dropped the bag of groceries. A can of tuna fish and two cans of peas rolled onto the path as the bag broke.

Suddenly she screamed. "I dropped the pills!" She got down on her hands and knees and began to search in the dense undergrowth.

Quickly Annie tied Flanagan's leash around a scrub oak and said, "Stay!" She knelt and looked for the pills, afraid Flanagan would find one and gulp it down, and maybe it would kill him or make him crazy.

The woman was frantic. "I got to have them. I can't make it if I quit 'em altogether."

After a few minutes Annie said, "Here's one."

"Oh, God bless you." The woman grabbed it, put it carefully back in the bottle, and screwed on the top. But although they searched awhile longer, they couldn't find the other one in the thick carpet of dead leaves and debris.

Finally the woman sat back on her heels. "Well, never mind. I'll keep looking. It's here someplace."

Annie thought about the old hibachi in the hut. "Do you light fires and cook and all?"

" 'Course I do. I have to have a cup of tea, don't I?"

"Isn't it dangerous? I mean, if you're not well . . ."

"You mean if I'm crazy. Say what you mean. Well, we all take chances, don't we?"

Annie nodded, but she knew she couldn't leave this woman here going out of her mind, building fires, maybe burning herself up. She looked at the bottle in Cora's hand and an idea hit her. "Look, why don't you give me the prescription number of your medication, and I'll get it refilled."

The woman looked at her. "Are you trying to trap me?"

Annie reacted impatiently. "If I wanted to trap you, I'd just go tell the police where you are. I'd have told them already."

The woman thought about it. "Well, you got a point. But they wouldn't refill it for you. You're just a kid."

"I've got a friend. My father is the priest at Saint Aidan's Church." She watched the woman's face for a reaction, but she didn't see one. Maybe Cora didn't remember having gone there. "And his curate is a good friend of mine. He's a young guy. He knows ways to help people that nobody else would think of. He could get it refilled, I bet."

The woman went into the shed and put her groceries on the ground. "Why don't you untie that poor dog?" she said.

"I'm afraid he'll find the pill and eat it."

"Oh." She stood in the doorway, her small, plump fists on her hips. "You got a pencil?"

Annie searched her jeans pockets. She always had a pencil, but she had no paper. Cora tore a piece off the grocery sack, gave it to Annie, and read off the prescription number. "Dr. MacKenzie. Up at the hospital."

"I need your last name."

"Hardy." She watched Annie write it down. "Why you going to this trouble?"

"I don't want anything to happen to you."

"What do you care?"

"I don't know."

"I 'spose it's because your old man is a priest."

"I don't think that has anything to do with it. You know, you don't make it all that easy to help you."

Cora laughed. The sound was like metal hitting metal. "You know what the shrinks tell us. If you do good for somebody, it's to make yourself feel good."

"Well, they must be wrong, because it's not making me feel a bit good." Annie untied Flanagan's leash.

"Hey, don't go away mad."

"Who said I was mad," Annie said, without looking back. As she and Flanagan turned off the path and out of sight, she heard Cora's laugh again.

"I guess she can't help it," Annie said to Flanagan, "but that Cora Hardy is a very irritating woman."

And if she was going to ask Benny to get the medication, she'd have to tell him about Cora. Well, fine. Let him worry about her.

It was starting to rain. They'd have to eat their picnic lunch at home in the kitchen.

chapter 15

She didn't call Benny when she got home. She had to think about this Cora business. She'd have to talk to him eventually because he was the only one she could think of who could get the pills, and obviously Cora ought to have them, even if she wouldn't take them regularly. The woman ought not to be there alone in that condition. Annie felt responsible for her.

"I'm not ready for this," she told Flanagan as she gave him his supper. "Being responsible for an adult, and an adult that's out of her mind besides."

During dinner Malcolm commented on how quiet she was.

"I'm beat," she said. "We had kind of a strenuous day, and then we got soaked coming home." It was still raining.

It was Robert's turn to help her clear away the dinner dishes and load the dishwasher.

"Rob," she said. She leaned against the sink, watching the rain streak the glass.

"Yeah?"

"Do you know anything about mental illness?"

He leaned against the counter with a dish of butter in his hands. A nice thing about Robert was that he always gave you his full attention if you asked him something serious. "Not really. I've got a friend who has Down's Syndrome."

"You have? Who?"

"Donny Farnham. He lives out past Four Corners, outside the town limits. His dad is a plumber."

"How did you get to know him?"

He shrugged. "I was just riding my bike, and I saw him, and we talked. I go to see him pretty often. I'm trying to teach him to play checkers, but he won't sit still very long."

She looked at him in wonder. "I never even knew you knew a boy like that. There's a lot I don't know about you."

"It'd be boring if we knew all about each other." He put the butter in the refrigerator.

"Is Down's Syndrome like being crazy?"

"Oh, no. It's more like being retarded, only different. Something in his head doesn't work right. He can't concentrate very well. He's a real nice kid. Why do you want to know about all that?"

She told him all about Cora. "It's a secret," she said, but she knew she didn't need to tell him that.

"If you tell Benny, it won't stay a secret. He'll have to do something."

"I don't have to say where she is."

"Come on. How long do you think it'll take him to find out? The arboretum is one of the places you take Flanagan, and it's the best place in town to hide. I've thought about hiding out in that old toolshed myself."

"You have?"

"Sure, when I was mad at Father. It'd make a neat hideout."

"Cora ought to be taking her medicine every day, but she doesn't do it even when she has enough. She says it makes her feel awful."

"Like me and penicillin," Robert said. "If she had a good doctor, he'd change the dose or get another medicine. Is she schizo or what?"

"I don't know. Manic-depressive, schizo—I don't even know what they mean, really."

Robert reached for the dictionary that their mother kept on the shelf with her cookbooks, and he flipped through the pages. " 'Manic-depressive: characterized by alternating mania and depression.' That's a big help." He turned to the S's. " 'Schizocarp: a dry compound fruit that splits at maturity into several indehiscent one-seeded carpels.' " He looked up. "What's *indehiscent*? What's a *carpel*?"

Annie had watched Robert look up words often enough to know how easily he was distracted by other words. "*Schizophrenia*," she reminded him.

"Yeah, I'm coming to it. *Schizomycete, schizomycosis*—

here we are. 'Schizophrenia: a type of psychosis characterized by loss of contact with environment and by disintegration of personality.' " He looked up. "Does that fit?"

She shook her head. "I don't know. I guess you'd have to be a psychiatrist to know."

"If then." Robert put the dictionary back. "Benny took a bunch of psych courses in college. He might have some idea. I wonder what *indehiscent* means." He took down the dictionary again.

Annie left him engrossed in the dictionary. Once he started looking up words, she'd lost him. She went out to say good-night to Flanagan and to make sure he was warm and dry in his house. It was raining hard now, and there were rumbles of thunder and flashes of lightning off to the east. The wind was chilly.

In her room she stripped off her clothes and put on flannel pajamas for the first time all summer. She got into bed with Judy Blume's *Tiger Eyes*, which was one of her favorite books. But tonight she couldn't concentrate on reading.

Robert was right that Benny would guess where Cora was hiding out. It wouldn't take a genius to figure it out. Then she would have broken her promise to Cora, because Benny would certainly do something about her, put her in some kind of hospital or halfway house or something. And that was what she was running away from. Cora was the kind of problem her father shrank from and Benny liked to try to solve. Maybe they were really a good combination. If you asked her father for comfort in distress, he'd quote Scripture to you. If you asked Benny, he'd get you to a therapist. Well, she'd *have* to talk to Benny tomorrow after church. She couldn't deal with it alone.

A crash of thunder sounded very close, and while it was still echoing, lightning lit up her room. It made her tingle. And then the lights went out.

She wriggled down under the bedclothes. She ought to get up to make sure all the windows were closed, but she didn't want to move. She had checked them before dinner, but somebody might have opened one. Oh, that's silly, she told herself; why would they? She hoped Flanagan wasn't scared.

She thought of Cora. That shed probably leaked like a sieve. It was a good thing Cora had that coat. And if she lighted the hibachi, it would be too wet to start any fires. But she'd fill the shed with smoke. Exasperated, Annie turned her pillow over and tried to find a comfortable place to burrow into. She was not going to lie awake all night worrying about Cora. Especially since there was not one blessed thing she could do.

Two hours later the lights came on, waking her up. I'll have to tell Benny, even though he'll know where she is, she thought. Winter's coming. She could die out there.

chapter 16

"Where's Mal?" Robert asked as he and Annie started to walk to church. The rain had stopped, but the sky was still overcast and there was a chilly wind.

"He went early. He's an acolyte today." She waved to Mrs. Ashley. "He wouldn't be seen walking with me, anyway."

"When you're in high school, you won't walk with me," Robert said.

"Of course I will."

"No, you won't. I've watched other people. High school kids act as if anybody younger doesn't exist, especially if it's a relative."

"You're crazy."

"No, I'm not. It's a stage. When you're in college, you'll remember me again. We'll probably be good friends."

"Robert!" Annie felt defensive because she knew he might be right. "We'll always be friends."

"Sure, basically. Hey, if it rains, I won't have to go to the Danielses' pool tomorrow. By the way, Ruthie said come over if you want to swim."

"Thanks a million. If she wants me, she can ask me." Annie was only half paying attention to the conversation. She was thinking about Flanagan, left alone in the rain. And she was thinking about Cora. Benny probably couldn't get the prescription filled on a Sunday, but they would have to do something about her. It was going to be a cold, wet night. She knew he worked sometimes with social services people in Salem and some of the other towns. He'd know what to do.

"How does she wash?" Robert said.

"Who?"

"The lady in the toolshed. How does she brush her teeth and all?"

She probably doesn't, Annie thought, but she didn't like to say that; it sounded unkind. "In the river, I guess."

"It's probably polluted. Everything's polluted now."

They were coming into the driveway of the church. Mrs. Parsons and Mrs. Evans waylaid them.

"I meant to call you children to see how you were getting along with your parents gone."

"Oh, we're fine, thanks," Annie said.

"Your mother is very trusting," Mrs. Evans said, smiling her Silly Putty smile. "Goodness, I'd never leave my kids alone in the house for three days."

Annie wanted to say, "Neither would I, if I had kids like yours," but she just smiled.

"What a pity about your dog," Mrs. Parsons said.

Annie looked at her, startled. "What about him?"

"Why, that you had to get rid of him."

"I didn't get rid of him."

"But the paper said he'd caused terrible trouble."

They were going up the steps into the church. Annie held the big oak door to let them go in first. "The paper was wrong."

Mrs. Evans and Mrs. Parsons exchanged looks and went into the church.

"Witches," Robert said under his breath.

The organist was playing softly while the congregation arrived. As they sat down in their pew near the front, they heard the roar of Benny's motorcycle coming down the street. They grinned at each other. Ben often got in just under the wire.

It was a good thing Malcolm was an acolyte today. If Ben forgot anything, Malcolm would take care of it if he possibly could. One of the things Ben and Annie's father clashed over was Father MacDougal's insistence on precision in the service and Ben's tendency to be careless. When Father MacDougal first came, he and the organist had worked out an arrangement: If anything went amiss that Father MacDougal hadn't noticed, Mrs. Altman, the organist, would softly play the opening notes of "The Campbells Are Coming," with lots of thrills and flourishes to disguise it. Then she would go smoothly into "A Mighty Fortress Is Our God." On the rare occasions when Ben took the service alone, he always panicked when he heard those notes, and his first instinct was to clutch at his waist.

He usually wore a dark gray silk vest under his cassock, tucked inside his trousers, and he said the silk was so slippery, he always felt as if his trousers were falling down.

"Good luck, Benito," Robert murmured as Ben came into view, looking only slightly windblown.

Ben cast a swift glance over the congregation. He never could resist doing that, although Annie's father had told him it was not his job to "count the house."

Like the others, Annie sang the hymns, most of which she knew by heart, and went through the responses, but today her mind kept wandering. She kept pointing out to God that Cora was "even the least of these," and she needed looking after. "Please let Ben find her a nice comfortable halfway house where they'll be good to her and see that she takes her medicine." Maybe if the Thorazine had such terrible side effects, another doctor could change the dose or find some other medicine that wouldn't make her suffer so much. Annie and Rob had bad side effects from penicillin, and they had Medic Alert bracelets they were supposed to wear. Thinking of the bracelet reminded her that she had not gotten her ID bracelet back from Cora. She must do that; her father had given it to her, and she liked it.

The rain was streaking the stained-glass windows, making odd configurations of light and dark. She hoped Cora could keep dry. Maybe they could take her a raincoat when she and Benny went out there. Because, promise or no promise, she would eventually have to take Benny with her to rescue Cora. She couldn't stay there all winter, and only Ben would know where to take her. Sometimes the MacDougals had taken in needy people for a short time, like for Thanksgiving dinner or Christmas Eve, but Annie knew her father did it out of a sense of duty; he hated to have his household upset. And he would certainly take Cora right back to the hospital and scold them for dismissing her. She could just hear him. Maybe it *was* where she belonged, but she'd already spent all her adult life there, and Annie knew from things she had read in the paper that it was not a good place to be: overcrowded, understaffed, no proper recreational facilities; it was even worse since the original big building had had a bad fire. There must be some better place for Cora. Benny would know.

She brought her mind back to the service and joined in the reading of the psalm: ". . . though I walk in the midst of trouble, you keep me safe. . . ." She did hope Cora was safe.

When Benny came forward to read the announcements, you could feel the congregation perk up. You never knew what Benny would say in those few informal moments.

First he said, "Good morning," as if he had just discovered them. He always did that. People smiled and murmured, "Good morning."

From a slip of paper in his hand, he read off the time and day of the Women's Guild luncheon, the practice time for the softball team, the meeting time of the Altar Guild. He folded the paper and looked out at them. "And the last piece of news is, this boy is goin' fishin'. As soon as I shake the last hand of the last faithful member of this congregation, I am off to pick up my mom in South Boston and pack her on the back of my cycle, where she dearly loves to be. Then we'll zoom off to Lake . . . well, if I tell you, you might beat me up there and catch all the big ones. I'll tell you this much: It's in New Hampshire, and my mother will catch the biggest bass in the lake. She always does."

As the congregation's murmur of laughter rose, Annie looked at Robert in dismay. "I thought it was *next* week."

Robert shrugged. "They must have switched."

Annie heard hardly a word of Benny's sermon. Her mind was in a turmoil. If she told Benny about Cora now, he would feel he'd have to deal with it before he left. It could rob him of a couple of days, at least, and she knew he needed his vacation. But how was she going to deal with Cora by herself?

She made herself pay attention. Benny was talking about parents, contrasting what he called the American attitude of "How do you deal with them?" with the Oriental attitude of love and respect for their wisdom and experience. In college he had taken a year off to travel with a jazz combo, and somehow they had ended up in China for a few weeks. He often spoke of his experiences there.

He was talking about his own mother. Annie had met her, a stocky, blond, outspoken woman who radiated so much vitality, you'd think raising seven children, losing her husband young, losing a child to leukemia, and putting four others through college had been as easy as making her delicious pasta.

Annie tried to listen, but her mind kept coming back to Cora. The more she worried, the harder the rain came down. Several times lightning flashed, lighting up the church for a startling moment, and thunder crashed nearby. Benny had to stop once or twice till the thunder died down.

"God is giving me competition," he said.

Robert took a pencil from his pocket and wrote on the

back of the order of service, "Tell him about Cora before he goes."

"It will spoil his vacation," she wrote.

"He can deal with it."

Annie noticed Mrs. Ashley watching them and frowning in gentle disapproval. She didn't write any more.

She tried to weigh one plan against another. Probably he and her father had moved Benny's vacation up a week because Benny had to handle everything alone while Father was gone. It was not surprising that no one had told her.

Even if Benny stayed to help, what could he do before tomorrow? Everything would be closed on Sunday. Then he'd have to hang around till they found a place for Cora to stay, or even if he didn't *have* to, he would, because he was so conscientious about things like that.

If she tried to handle it alone, she probably could get the prescription filled tomorrow. She could phone in the number, try to sound grown up, and say it would be picked up later. No one was likely to cross-examine her about that. If it had to be checked out with the doctor for a refill, the pharmacist would call him, and she doubted that the doctors at the hospital had time to go into a lot of questions about patients who weren't even there anymore.

She'd have to look up social services agencies in the phone book. She knew about the one in Salem that Benny worked with, for kids in trouble or on drugs. But what if the agency people just sent Cora back to the hospital or to the Valenti person?

She fished in her jacket pocket for the envelope as Mr. Ainsley and Mr. LeBaron came up the aisle taking the collection.

During the celebration of the Eucharist, she tried to

keep her mind on the service, but the other thing on her mind was dinner. She hadn't thought to ask her mother if they would eat out somewhere on their way home. She wanted to have a good dinner ready for Sherry's homecoming, in case they came in tired and hungry. She'd waked up early and peeled potatoes and carrots and onions to go with the roast she had bought yesterday with her own money. Her father loved roast beef. She was going to make Yorkshire pudding, although that was tricky about the timing. She'd make a cake from a mix, and there was ice cream in the fridge. The problem was finding Cora and making sure she was warm and dry, and getting home in time to have the dinner ready at six.

Benny was standing looking out over the congregation now, making the sign of the cross and giving the benediction. He looked so serious and *good*, and she thought how much she loved him. She couldn't ruin his vacation with his nice mother.

At the door of the church, she stood with the others as they shook hands or hugged him and wished him a good vacation. He had a happy grin on his face. She couldn't dump problems on him now. She hugged him hard and said, "Catch a big one," and walked away. She was on her own.

chapter 17

"I'll go with you," Robert said.

"No, you stay here, and if I'm not back by four o'clock, please put the roast in the oven, three-hundred-fifty degrees. If you forget, it's right here in *The Joy of Cooking*." She had the cookbook open at the right page. "It's already in the roaster." She was piling things into a bundle inside a blue tarp: a warm sweater of her own, some wool socks, a can of baked beans, a can of roast-beef hash, half a bag of M&M's, a can of brown bread, some carrots—all things Cora could eat without cooking. "That ought to tide her over till I can get her moved somewhere tomorrow."

"Moved where?" Robert said. "Would she like a book to read?"

"I don't think so. Not right now. I don't know 'moved where.' I'm going to have to find a place for her."

Robert shook his head. "You ought to get Father to help."

"No. He'd send her back to the hospital."

"Maybe that's where she should be."

"They threw her out. They'd just send her back to Valenti."

"What's a Valenti?"

"Robert, I have to go. Listen, one more thing—would you check on Flanagan? I haven't even had time to speak to him."

"Don't worry. He's inside his little house. It is pouring buckets, you know."

"I know." She put on her windbreaker and an old rain hat that hung on a hook in the back hall and belonged to everybody. "See you later."

"I think you're out of your mind," he said. "You think you're Florence Nightingale or something."

She went out, carrying the bulky tarp, not bothering to answer. She didn't feel at all like Florence Nightingale or any kind of heroine, if that was what he meant. She felt miserable, and she wanted just to forget Cora entirely. But she couldn't. The only thing she felt good about was not having dumped it all on Ben.

It was hard riding her bike in the rain with the bundle of food and clothes balanced on the carrier. She kept skidding. The rain soaked her jeans and drove into her face, and she could taste the salt that told her it was an east wind, blowing off the ocean. It might be wet for a day or two. Maybe she could somehow attach the tarp to the earthen roof of the toolshed, although offhand she couldn't think how. Well, she'd cross that bridge when she got to it.

A car passed, throwing up a drenching spray. She kept her head down, not wanting to be recognized. If there was anything she didn't need, it was some kindhearted parishioner stopping to ask what she was doing.

Even riding the bike instead of walking, it seemed twice as far to the arboretum as it ever had before. As she turned into the woods, her bike skidded in a mud puddle, and the tarp-wrapped bundle flew off. She tried to wipe the mud off, then decided to let the rain do it. She walked her bike over the bumpy path, wishing Flanagan were with her.

Maybe Cora would be gone. What a relief that would be: the whole business taken out of her hands. Only then she'd have to worry about where she had gone. Did people go through life worrying about other people all the time, or was she some kind of neurotic? A worrywart, her mother called her. And her father had added that worrywarts could turn into meddlers. Was she meddling in Cora's life, or was she helping? She hadn't the faintest idea. Whatever it was, she wished she were home in the kitchen with Flanagan, making a salad and smelling the roast beef cooking. She hoped she'd get it done enough for Father; he was so fussy.

She'd hardly had time to think about Sherry, but it would be nice to have her back, even if she did go dancing all over the house like some kind of sprite, knocking things over and never picking them up. Robert wouldn't allow her in his room since the day she accidentally scattered the pages of a story he'd been working on, mixing up the revised with the original pages. Well, that was Sherry.

She turned into the path leading to the toolshed and shuddered as a big pine branch dumped its load of rain down the back of her neck. She tried to see ahead of her, but it was impossible; the rain was like a gray curtain blowing in her face.

The door to the toolshed was closed. She shifted the bundle to her left shoulder and knocked. "Miss Cora? It's me, Annie."

Silence. Her hopes rose. If Cora wasn't there, she could just leave her bundle inside the door, in case she came back, and ride home as fast as possible. She knocked again. "Miss Cora? It's Annie MacDougal."

Very slowly the door opened a crack, then a little wider.

"It's just me," Annie said.

The door opened farther, scraping against the wet earth. "Come in," Cora said.

I should have thought of a flashlight, Annie said to herself. It was very dark inside the cave. "I thought you might be having trouble keeping dry. I brought a waterproof tarp and a few things." She put the bundle on the dirt floor and opened it up. The shed smelled of wine. Wine? Was Cora going to turn out to be an alcoholic along with everything else? Annie tried to focus on her face in the dim light.

"That was real nice." Cora's voice was calm, lower-pitched, without the undertone of hysteria that had been there that one time. "I like baked beans," she said.

"I brought things you could eat without making a fire. If you don't mind cold food."

"My mama always said if you're hungry enough, you won't be too fussy."

"I brought a can opener, but I guess you have one."

"I lost it," Cora said.

Annie tried to make out the difference in her face. It was hard to see details in the gloom, but Cora did look different. Her hair was combed. Her face was washed. "Did you ever find that pill we were looking for?"

"I did. I looked and looked, and I found it rolled in under a bunch of pine needles. I took it last night." She shuddered. "It was a real bad night. But I feel better now."

She seemed to Annie to be almost normal. If that was what medication could do, they would certainly have to find some kind that worked without making her suffer from the side effects. "You look better."

"Let's open the beans," Cora said. "I've got a couple of plastic spoons; they give you these when you buy a cup of coffee at the convenience store. That's what they call those places, convenience stores."

"Yes." Annie wished she'd thought to bring a thermos of coffee.

"I been collecting rainwater to drink," Cora said. "Purest water there is. We always had a rain barrel outside our cellar door."

Annie thought of acid rain, but she didn't say anything. She opened the can of beans and gave it to Cora, then shook her head when Cora offered her some. "I can't stay very long. My family is coming home from a trip and I have to fix dinner for them." She paused. "But I'll come back tomorrow. I'm going to find you some decent place to stay."

Cora looked up quickly. "Hospital?"

"No, no, of course not. I promise. I don't know just what yet, but I'm going to ask around."

"There's no kind of place except like Valenti's, and I'm not going there. I'm all right here."

Annie pointed to the water streaking the sides of the shed. "We could be getting a nor'easter. It could pour for days. You could get flooded out here."

Cora set her jaw in a stubborn line. "I'm not leaving. I'm safe here."

"It's going to get cold in a few weeks."

"A few weeks I'm not worrying about." She ate some more beans. "My mother used to bake good beans, all day long on top of the stove, real slow, with a hunk of salt fat pork."

"How long ago did your mother die?"

Cora looked bewildered. "I don't know. The shocks make you lose your memory."

For a moment Annie thought she meant the shock of losing her mother. Then she realized she meant the shock treatments.

"I get things mixed up. I lost a lot of time in there somewhere."

"Well, that's all right." Annie was sorry she had asked. It had upset Cora. "How about if I spread the tarp over the ground here, where it's getting soggy? Then you can sit on it and keep dry. It's big enough to wrap around you. I brought a sweater."

Cora's eyes filled with tears. "You're a good kid. Nobody's been nice to me since Mama died."

Annie didn't know what to say. What did Ben say when people needed comforting?

They both turned quickly as the door to the shed was pushed farther open. Cora held the can of beans against her chest as if for protection.

"Anybody home?"

"Ben!" Annie couldn't believe it. "I thought you'd gone."

"I stopped by the house, and Robert gave me the dope. Can I come in? Is there room?" He stooped and came inside. "Raining like cats and dogs out there. Hello, you must be Miss Cora." His raincoat dripped on the edge of the tarp, making tiny sounds.

Cora had moved as far back as she could get. "You sold me out," she said to Annie.

"I didn't, honestly." Annie felt half frightened, half relieved. She wanted Cora to trust her. But now she could let Benny take over.

"No, she kept her promise to you, Miss Cora. I just happened to hear about you by chance. I'm Father Ben Vitale. I'm assistant to Annie's father at the church. I think you were there one night when I was doing Vespers."

"You're going to take me back to the hospital." She picked up the can opener and held it like a weapon.

"No way. I worked one summer in a hospital like that, when I was in seminary."

"I won't go back to Valenti."

"You don't have to go anywhere you don't want. I'm going away for a week, and I thought you might like to stay in my house till I get back. Then we'll find a good place for you."

"Your house?" Cora looked puzzled.

Annie was alarmed. She wanted to warn Benny that Cora was not always as calm as she seemed today. She wished she could talk to him alone for a few minutes. She wondered how much Robert had told him.

The wind was blowing hard, and a branch was beating against the shed, making it hard to talk. She wondered if they were going to get an early hurricane.

"I talked to a friend of mine just before I came out here. She's a nurse, but she's retired, a great gal. You'll like her. She offered to stay with you while I'm gone." He looked at her. "What do you say?"

"It's up to me?"

"Sure. Nobody's going to force you. My house is small, and it's kind of short on furniture, and the bathroom faucet drips, but the freezer's full of food, and if you like to read, there are plenty of books."

Cora looked at Annie. "Is it a trap?" She held out her hand as if for help, and Annie saw her ID bracelet on Cora's wrist.

"No," Annie said gently. "Father Ben is the most honest man I know, and the kindest."

"You're the only one ever helped me," Cora said. "In all this rain and wind, I got to trust you." She looked at Ben. "I accept."

"Great. Let's get your things together and get this show on the road."

Cora laughed unexpectedly, a rusty sound. "That's what my mother used to say: Let's get this show on the road."

Ben and Annie were already gathering up Cora's few things, packing some of them in the tarp, some in the paper grocery bags Cora had saved.

"What's this?" Annie held up a small statuette of a girl on skates. It was too dark to read the inscription.

Cora grabbed it. "That's my trophy. I got that for figure skating, when I was eighteen."

"Really?" Ben sounded genuinely interested. "I love to watch figure skaters on TV. I always wanted a pair of skates when I was a kid. I thought I'd inherit my sister's, but she gave them to a cousin of ours."

"Skating is like flying," Cora said. "You fly through the air like a bird."

Annie looked at the bent figure and tried to imagine her young and flying on skates. How could people change so much?

"We'll have to pick up your little stove later," Ben said. "Okay?"

"Sure. Don't work good, anyway."

When they had everything packed, they started down the path, Ben shielding Cora under his raincoat with his arm around her. The wind had increased. Annie balanced the loaded tarp on the seat of the bike, following blindly behind Ben. She hoped he hadn't come on his motorcycle.

It was her father's station wagon that was parked at the entrance. He helped Cora into the front seat and loaded Annie's bike into the back, where she sat surrounded by Cora's belongings, wondering how all this was going to work.

She leaned forward to speak to Ben as he turned the wagon around. "Cora needs her prescription refilled. She just took her last pill."

"All but one," Cora said. "I got one left."

"No problem," Ben said. "Myrt can get it."

"It's a Salem drugstore."

"Myrt can call it in today, and they'll put it in the

mail. She'll have it in the morning. They may be closed, but there's always an emergency number for the pharmacist."

Those were the things Ben knew. She needn't have worried about the prescription after all. If you were going to care about what happened to other people, you needed to know stuff like that.

Ben turned on the windshield wipers as the old station wagon rocked and bumped along. "Just one promise I'm going to ask of you, Cora," he said.

"Here it comes," Cora said.

"Yeah, the kicker. But I think it's fair. I'm going to ask you to take your medication on schedule. All right?"

Cora didn't answer. She was huddled in the seat, shapeless in her too-big overcoat, her light hair frizzled with rain.

After a minute Ben said, "Because when I come back, I want to know I can rely on you for that, when I go looking for a place for you to live."

"Halfway house?" she said.

"Not unless we find one you like. It's going to be you that decides. So you'll need to be in good shape, like you are now."

She laughed her harsh little guffaw again. "Don't look to me like I'm what you'd call good-shaped. Not in this coat. I found this coat in a trash can. Can you believe it? Throwing away a perfectly good coat?"

She hadn't given the promise, and Ben didn't push her. He was treating her the same way he treated everybody, not as if she was sick or different in any way.

He dropped off Annie at her house. "I'll be in touch."

"What about your trip?"

"Just delayed a few hours. I'll call Mom. She's used to me being late." He grinned. "You all are."

"Cora, I'll come over to see you tomorrow," Annie said. "I'll make a cake. We'll have a party."

Cora smiled. "That'll be nice."

When Annie went into the house, Flanagan bounded up from his position near the stove and wagged his tail wildly, rubbing his head against her wet clothes. Robert was sitting at the kitchen table with a pen in his hand and a legal pad in front of him. He looked up abstractedly.

"What are you doing in the kitchen?" Annie asked him. The roast beef was on top of the stove, and she noticed the timer was set.

"I'm working on my book, and I was afraid I'd forget about the roast, so I set the timer. And Flanagan wanted to come in. How'd it go out there?"

"I'm glad you told Ben."

"I was afraid you'd be mad."

"No, I couldn't have done anything without him. He's going to leave her in his house while he's gone."

"I know. He called Myrtle Blanchard from here. Will it be okay? She won't wreck the place or anything? Is she very ditsy?"

"She's not like that. When she takes her medicine, she's like anybody else. Or almost."

"Well, Myrtle can handle her. You're sopping wet. You better take a hot shower."

She grinned. "Yes, Mother." She felt as if a great iron yoke had been taken off her shoulders. "If Ben calls while I'm in the shower, tell him I'll visit Cora every afternoon so Myrtle can get out for a couple of hours." She rubbed Flanagan's coat. "You stay here. I won't be long."

In the shower she turned the water on as hot as she could stand it and let her tensed-up muscles relax. Outside the rain pounded against the house, and the wind rattled the shutters.

chapter 18

"The roast is very good, Daughter," Annie's father said.

Annie beamed. Father's praise was rare. "Is the Yorkshire pudding okay?"

"Everything's wonderful, dear," her mother said.

"It beats camp food." Sherry, looking tanned and taller, jumped up and danced out to the kitchen to give Flanagan a hug.

"Stay in your chair, please," her father said. But he did not sound stern. Both parents had been impressed with Sherry's solo in the recital, and for the first time her father was speaking of her dancing as if it were more than a childish whim.

"Were you really any good, Sher?" Malcolm asked. "How many times did you fall down?"

"She didn't fall once," his father said. "She was splendid. Really quite splendid." He looked bemused, as if he could hardly believe he had sired this dancing sprite.

Annie saw the look and felt depressed. He would never look that way about her. When she went out to the kitchen to get more salad, Flanagan leaped to his feet. He had been allowed to stay in the kitchen because of the weather. "Not yet," she told him. "Mother said you can spend the night in my room because we may get a hurricane. So be patient. Lie down." She pushed him down. He was getting to be very obedient.

The phone rang, and Malcolm jumped up to answer it. Nothing had been said about Cora and Ben. Malcolm had been at a friend's house and had missed the whole thing. She would have to tell her parents, of course, now that things had progressed this far, but she wanted to wait till tomorrow. She would tell her mother first, and let her tell Father.

In a few minutes Malcolm came back to the table looking puzzled.

"Who was it?" Robert said.

"Man, that's really weird," Malcolm said.

"What's weird?" Annie said. She hoped it hadn't been Cora.

"You know that kid that beat me out for the county title?"

"Of course we know," Robert said. "So what?"

"That was him."

"*He*," his mother said.

"He invited me over for dinner tomorrow. His family has a tennis court."

"That's nice," his mother said. "He lives in Manchester, doesn't he? Your father or I will drive you over there."

"But we're enemies. Why should he ask me over?"

"Probably wants to poison your Coke," Robert said.

"Opponents are not enemies," his father said. "He defeated you in a fair match."

"But that's why I hate him."

Annie wanted to laugh. Malcolm always got himself in trouble by being too honest.

"Did he clobber you, Mal?" Sherry asked.

"Never mind," her mother said. "Eat your salad."

Annie's mind was only half on the family scene. She was thinking about Cora. She tried to picture her bathed and shampooed, wrapped in Benny's old bathrobe, watching TV with Myrt. Or was it like that? Maybe she was confused and upset again.

Later, when she was in her room, she lay on her bed thinking about Cora and thinking about the skinheads that had roared into town. Violence in this quiet town was so unexpected, it seemed somehow more frightening than . . . well, than when you saw it on TV. Although that was bad enough.

She lay still, trying to relax, her radio turned low. Sherry's half of the room was strewn with clothes, ballet shoes, tutus, leotards, pictures of camp and friends, half-full packs of bubble gum. Sherry was never neat, and when she was unpacking from a trip, her part of the room looked as if that hurricane they were talking about on the radio had just struck.

In fact, the weather report was optimistic about the

hurricane. It was supposed to head out to sea after it hit the Carolinas.

"I'm glad we're all inside," Annie said to Flanagan, who was stretched out on the floor with his head against the bed. "I hope they don't get a big wind in Boothbay Harbor. The Meyerses have a couple of boats up there." She put her hand on his head. "They'll be coming home soon, and they're going to be proud of you. You've gotten so good, and you look so beautiful."

Sherry pirouetted into the room. "Oh, it's fun to be home. Flanagan, come over here with me."

Annie had anticipated this. "No," she said. "I'm sorry. Flanagan stays here."

"Oh, you're going to be selfish," Sherry said.

"Yes," Annie said firmly. "I am."

chapter 19

In spite of the soothing words of the weatherman, the next day brought gale-force winds. Annie had intended to go to Ben's house to make sure Cora was all right and to give Myrt a break, but as she was eating breakfast, her mother came into the kitchen and said, "You have a message from Myrtle Blanchard that might as well be in Greek for all I understand of it. But here it is." She consulted a small telephone notepad. " 'Tell Annie not to think of coming over in this weather. All is fine here. Cora took her medication and had a rough night, but I sat up and held her hand. Today she's fine. We are playing a wild game of checkers for a penny a point. She's wearing your nice warm sweater. I'll call you tomorrow.' " Annie's mother looked at her. "I thanked her politely. Would you care to translate? Who is Cora? Why is she wearing your sweater? What is Myrt doing? Or is it all one of those mysteries mothers never find out about?"

"I was planning to tell you. You'd better sit down. It's a long story."

"Wait till I get a cup of coffee."

When her mother was settled, Annie told her about Cora—all of it, starting with Ben's seeing her in the back of the church.

Her mother listened in growing amazement. "And you never told a soul?"

"Only Robert."

She nodded. "Your alter ego. And he told Ben. Well, thank fortune he did. I shudder to think, if you had tried to deal with all that by yourself. Why didn't you tell your father?"

"I was afraid he would say she should go to the hospital or the halfway house."

"Yes, I expect he would." She studied her daughter's face. "That was a lot to undertake. I'm proud of you."

"You are?" Annie was surprised. She had expected at least a mild scolding for taking things into her own hands, for deceiving everybody, or whatever.

"I would say you were a Good Samaritan, except that I've just been reading a book Ben lent me on interpretations of the parables, and I think I won't." She put her hand on Flanagan's head. "Flanagan, you were really the one who found this Cora person. You deserve credit, too. Now, Annie, what in the world is Ben going to do with her?"

"He'll think of something."

"Don't expect miracles. Ben is only human, although I know you tend to think otherwise."

"I know he's human, but he knows everybody, and he knows how to do things."

Her mother sipped her coffee, frowning thoughtfully. "Cora sounds schizophrenic, doesn't she?"

"I don't know. Robert and I looked it up in the dictionary, but it didn't help much."

"Something you have to face, no matter how well things can be worked out, is that Cora won't get better. Schizophrenia usually gets worse."

"Even with medication?"

"The medication may make it a little easier to bear. If the medication works. And sometimes the side effects are dreadful."

"Cora said hers were."

"I'm sure Ben will find her a good doctor, at least. The doctors at state hospitals, even if they are good, are overworked and underfunded; all they can do is try to keep the lid on."

"How come you know so much about mental illness? Does everybody?"

"One of my best friends developed schizophrenia right after high school."

"Oh. You never told me."

"No. She died in the hospital, in another state. She wandered outside on a bitter cold night. No one missed her till morning. She froze to death." She sat very still for a moment and then shook her head. "It probably would have happened to Cora if you hadn't found her. How lucky she stumbled on that old toolshed. We're going to have to tell your father about this, you know."

"Will you tell him?"

"If you want." She paused. "Are you afraid of your father, Annie?"

"Not really, but he has such strong ideas."

There was an explosion of noise as Sherry and Malcolm arrived at the top of the stairs at the same moment.

"Never mind," Sherry shrieked. "I'll slide down the banister."

There was a thump a moment later that made her mother wince.

Robert drifted downstairs after Malcolm, looking sleepy.

"Hey," Malcolm said to Robert, "you didn't even tell us, did you win the freestyle Saturday?"

"Nope. I came in second. Tony won."

Malcolm studied his brother. "You act like you don't even care."

"I don't."

"If you compete and you don't care if you win or lose, what's the point?"

Robert shrugged. "If he wrote a better story than I did, I'd hate his guts."

Father MacDougal came into the kitchen. "I believe I'll go to the church and work on my sermon. Do you know where my raincoat is?"

"It's blowing a gale outside," his wife said.

"Inside this house it's a hurricane." He took the coat that she brought him from the back hall and found a wide-brimmed hat and clapped it on his head. "If Noah could survive, perhaps I can." Laboriously he pulled on a pair of rubbers, kissed his wife, and left, letting in a blast of wind and rain.

His wife watched him struggle against the wind to the garage. " 'Much buffeted he on land and sea,' " she murmured. "Was that Virgil, or was it Caesar? Virgil, I think."

"Bacon and eggs, Mama?" Malcolm said. "Pancakes?"

"French toast," Sherry said. She spun around the room on her toes. "With maple syrup." She threw her arms around Flanagan. "Flanagan and I are going to play all day. We'll go for a nice walk."

"You will not," her mother said.

Annie pried Sherry loose from Flanagan and led him upstairs. She heard Sherry say, "Mama, why is Annie so selfish about that dog?"

"Because it's her dog," her mother said.

"I thought we shared around here."

"My darling, your idea of sharing is taking over. Now sit down and drink your juice."

chapter 20

The storm gradually lessened during the day. Annie had stayed in her room with Flanagan, reading. Robert was trying to draw an acceptable version of an Irish wolfhound, and Malcolm kept calling the weather channel, afraid that it would be too stormy for anyone to take him to his tennis rival's house for dinner. Sherry spent most of the day talking to her friends on the phone.

When Malcolm and his mother left, Malcolm tossed the soggy *Chronicle* in the door. Sherry was reading the comic page when Annie came downstairs. She had almost forgotten about the retraction the editor had promised, but there it was, in small print at the bottom of the front page, as he had promised: "Correction: Our story last week about Anne MacDougal's dog contained certain factual errors, which we regret. There is no police investigation."

"For whatever good that does," Annie said. She clipped it out carefully to save for Benny. "At least I've been promoted to my real name instead of my nickname."

Since it would be another hour or so before her mother began to fix dinner, Annie decided to make the cake she had promised Cora. Tomorrow she would take it over there, and they would have a little tea party. Myrt could get out if she wanted a change, or she could stay. Annie hoped she'd stay. Cora wasn't easy to talk to, at best.

When her father came home and was sipping his sherry in the living room, Annie showed him the clipping.

"I wish you wouldn't cut up the paper before I read it," was all he said. One of his parishioners had interrupted him in his study at the parish hall, and he had had to listen to her complaints about her husband when he wanted to be working on his sermon. He was not in the best of moods. Annie was glad it was Robert's turn to provide a topic for dinner.

He held the damp newspaper at arm's length, trying to read it without his glasses. "They're having a special town meeting next week," he said.

"What about?" Annie's mother sat down with a cup of tea. She had just come home from delivering Malcolm to his host's house.

"Oh, there seem to be half-a-dozen special warrants. Something about John Peters's septic tank. Something about the allotment for snow removal." He held the paper a little farther away and squinted at it. "The usual brouhaha about using the old junior high school for a private Christian Evangelical school, i.e., should they lease it, sell it, or forget it." He threw the paper on the floor. "One would think that paperboy could get one's paper to one's door in a readable condition." He sneezed. "Where is the dog?"

"In his run," Annie said quickly.

"I hope you're not catching a cold, Dougal," his wife said. "You'd better have another dab of sherry."

"I never catch cold," he said, but he held out his glass for the extra sherry.

At dinner Robert's topic was superconductivity, and since not even his father knew much about it, Robert held forth, slipping easily from the facts about magnetism to a vivid picture of Americans abandoning their cars and going everywhere at almost the speed of light in the new magnetic trains.

"Robert, dear, you do embellish," his mother said.

"That's one word for it," his father said. "I suppose we may expect a science-fiction novel from you on the subject."

Robert grinned. "Maybe someday."

"I don't know what any of you are talking about," Sherry said. "I wish sometimes you'd talk about sensible things."

"Well, tomorrow it's your turn." Her father's grim look lightened.

She's his favorite child, Annie thought.

"Maybe you could get magnetic ballet shoes," Robert said, "and dance higher and faster than anybody in the world."

Sherry looked interested. "Really?"

"He's teasing," her mother said. "Eat your lettuce."

The cake Annie had baked came out well, and she hid it where her brothers wouldn't find it.

Even so, she was rather surprised to find it still there the next day. In the morning she took Flanagan to the meadow for the first time since the unpleasant encounter with the children. Mrs. Anderson, leaning on her side of the fence, watched her go, hoping, Annie thought, that we get into trouble.

Nothing happened along the way except that they met Mrs. Evans, who gave them a smile and shied away from Flanagan as if he were a wild animal.

Once Annie had to use her strength to keep Flanagan from chasing an orange cat, but otherwise he behaved very well. In the meadow they went through the obedience exercises, and he seemed to remember them all.

"Good dog!" she told him. "I'm proud of you. You must have a high IQ."

When she took him home, she put him in the run and told him that she would be gone for a while. "I have to go see Cora," she told him. "You remember Cora. You were the one who found her. But I don't think I'd better take you with me. Benny's place is small."

She told Sherry she could play ball with Flanagan in the run if she wanted to. "But remember to latch the gate when you leave. Don't forget, Sherry."

"Boss, boss, boss," Sherry said. But she smiled. "I'll play nice with him, Annie."

When she was finishing her lunch, her father came into the kitchen. "That's a fine-looking cake," he said. "Does one get a piece?"

"Oh, Father, I'm sorry. This one is for Cora. I'll make another one when I get home."

He sat down across from her, taking off his glasses. "We have not discussed the business of the woman called Cora."

"No." Annie felt nervous. She knew her mother had told him the whole story, but he had not mentioned it.

"I am pleased that you were moved to compassion by this poor creature's plight, but I wonder why you didn't come to me about it."

Annie brushed some crumbs into her plate. There was no way she could answer his question except with the truth. "I thought you would take her back to the hospital."

"Annie, when people are sick, they belong in the hospital."

"They threw her out. They put her in a halfway house, where the woman in charge was cruel to her."

He stroked his chin. "So she says. People who are ill as this woman is are usually paranoid. You understand what *paranoid* means?"

She sighed. She wished he wouldn't patronize her. "Yes, Father, I know what *paranoid* means, and I thought of that with Cora. But I have seen the terror in her eyes. Even when she's medicated and relatively calm, the mention of . . ." She had been about to say "Valenti," but she didn't want her father tracking down Valenti's halfway house. He would do it thinking it was the right thing. ". . . even the mention of the house where she stayed frightens her very badly. It would be inhuman to make her go back there."

He frowned and took off his glasses. "But she must go somewhere."

"There are other halfway houses. Ben will find a good one."

He gave a sardonic sniff. "Ben is not the fount of all knowledge and wisdom, even though you seem to think so." After a pause he said, "I am not at all pleased that Ben has left this person in his house while he's away. Ben seems to have trouble understanding what is appropriate and what is not."

Annie's mother came in quietly, walking into the pantry, where she was out of sight.

"He had to think of someplace in a hurry," Annie said. "Is it inappropriate to provide shelter for a homeless, sick woman?" She hoped it sounded like an innocent question, not a challenge.

"People are very sensitive to having mentally unbalanced people in their backyards, so to speak."

"But it's only for a week. And Cora is harmless. Ben says many more mentally ill people are victims of violence than *do* violence."

He stood up, looking annoyed. "Ben says, Ben says! The church owns that house Ben lives in. I should have been consulted. I want that person out of there the minute Ben returns." He strode out of the kitchen.

Annie felt depressed. She hated to have her father angry with her, and even more, she hated to have him angry with Ben. In spite of what he had said, she was still sure that it would have been cruel to return Cora to either the hospital or Valenti's. There must be good places, and Ben would find one. She realized it was the first time she had ever taken a real stand against her father. Maybe it meant she was starting to grow up, but whatever it was, it was not easy.

She found a box to pack Cora's cake in. She had frosted it with mocha frosting, her own favorite, and she hoped Cora would like it.

Her mother came out of the pantry. She had been making a grocery list. "Think of anything we need at the IGA?"

Annie shook her head.

"I'll give you a ride to Ben's," her mother said.

"It's out of your way."

"Not more than a block or two. Are you ready to go?"

As they came out to the garage, Malcolm and another boy zoomed into the yard on bikes. Annie didn't recognize the other boy, about Malcolm's age, all long arms and legs and floppy blond hair.

"Mom, this is Ned," Malcolm said. "Can he stay to dinner?"

"Of course. I'm glad to know you, Ned." She reached out and shook his hand. He blushed. "This is Annie, Malcolm's sister."

"Hi, Ned," Annie said.

As she and her mother drove away, Annie said, "Is that the mortal enemy? The one Mal was going to massacree?"

"That's the one."

"He doesn't look dangerous."

"No. I'm glad they're friends. Your father is right about sportsmanship."

They drove in silence. Just before they reached Ben's

house, her mother said, "Sometimes, you know, women see things differently from men. Not necessarily more clearly, but differently."

Annie gave her mother a quick look. She knew she was talking about Cora.

"One has to make allowances for the differences," her mother went on. "Factor it in, so to speak. And then do what one has to do." She stopped in front of Ben's little house. A woman next door came out in the yard to see who was there; that was Mrs. Felton, the one Ben didn't get along with.

"Thanks," Annie said, reaching for the car door.

"I'm going to get my hair cut," her mother said.

"What!" Annie almost dropped the cake. "Why?"

Her mother had her hair braided in a heavy plait down her back. "The other day I saw a woman about my age with hair longer than mine. She looked ridiculous."

"But your beautiful hair."

"I'll still have some. It came to me suddenly that I'm not a hippie anymore. I'm a grown woman with four children, one of them starting to grow up herself."

Annie studied her mother's face. "Is it hard, growing up?"

"In my opinion, and strictly off the record, it's pure hell." Her mother smiled and patted her arm. "Look, Cora must need things, clothes and a toothbrush and that sort of thing. Why don't you make a list and give it to me tonight."

Annie nodded. Again she started to get out of the car. Then she turned to her mother. "I like you, Mom."

Her mother laughed. "Thanks. I like you, too. Say hi

to Myrt for me. Tell her if she wants a day off, I can make it Thursday."

Annie stood on the sidewalk watching her mother drive off. After a moment she realized that the Felton woman was speaking to her.

"Who are those people in Father Vitale's house?" she said.

"One of them is a nurse friend of ours, Myrtle Blanchard." She started up the walk, anxious to get away from this woman who, she knew, was nosy about her neighbors.

"Who's the other one?"

"A friend," Annie called back.

"Friend in a pig's foot," Mrs. Felton snapped. "She looks like one of those bag ladies. Personally, I think she's balmy."

Pretending not to have heard her, Annie ran up the steps and rang the doorbell. Then, remembering it didn't work, she knocked.

"Oh, good, it's you." Myrt looked tired. "Come in, darlin'. What have you brought us?" She raised her voice. "Cora, look who's here—your best buddy. And I think she's brought you a present." Under her breath she said, "Very depressed today. I think she spat out her pill. Yesterday she talked a blue streak all day, but today hardly a word can I get out of her. Ah, there you are, Cora. Look, here's Annie."

"I see her." Cora shuffled into the room, her shoulders bent. She looked as if she had been thoroughly washed and shampooed, her hair combed neatly. She was wearing a pair of Ben's old jeans, held up by a leather belt, and a white sweatshirt that said RED SOX on the front. Her small feet were hidden in Ben's fleece-lined slippers.

"I'm glad to see you, Cora." Annie felt shy, not sure of what to say.

Cora nodded. "Likewise." She sat down in Ben's recliner and jumped nervously when the footrest shot into place.

"I brought you a chocolate cake," Annie said. "With mocha frosting."

"Wow!" Myrt said, making an effort to sound enthusiastic. "We can have a tea party. How about a cup of nice herbal tea and a piece of Annie's cake, Cora?"

Cora shook her head. "Not hungry." She leaned her head back and closed her eyes.

Myrt and Annie exchanged looks. "Well, maybe a little later," Myrt said. "Cora didn't sleep much last night. She's kind of tired."

"You, too," Annie said. "If you'd like to go out for a while, I can stay. And my mother said she can come all day Thursday, if you want a day off."

"Bless her heart, that's one of the most thoughtful women God ever made. I may take her up on it. Listen, I *would* like to go down to the 7-Eleven and get me some candy bars. Since I quit smoking, I'm a chocaholic. I'm going to get fat as a pig."

Annie smiled. "Not likely. Listen, take your time. I don't have to be home till about five-thirty."

"I won't be long." Myrt searched for her purse.

"Mom's getting her hair cut."

"What! That gorgeous hair!"

"That's what *I* said. It's going to be a shock."

"Does your dad know it?"

"I doubt it."

"He'll need the last rites when he sees her. Well, it'll be a lot easier to take care of, I guess." She approached Cora's chair. "Cora, honey, I'm going out for a few minutes. Annie will be here. Anything I can get you? How about some ice cream?"

"Real ice cream?"

"You bet. Häagen-Dazs. What's your pleasure: chocolate almond? Espresso? Raspberry sorbet?"

"I haven't had ice cream for years. You pick one."

"All right. How about you, Annie?"

"Chocolate almond." Annie walked her to the door. "Is there anything special I should do?"

"No," Myrt said in a low voice. "Just be here. She won't have much to say. It looks to me like manic-depressive, but Ben called today and told me to get this doctor we both think a lot of. He's coming tomorrow. Poor soul. It breaks your heart. She's wearing your ID bracelet, by the way. You want me to get it back?"

"No, let her wear it." As Myrt opened the door, Annie said, "She used to be a champion skater."

"I know. She's got that trophy on the bureau. She likes to hold it. Dear God, it breaks your heart." She shook her head and went off at a fast walk.

Cora seemed to be asleep when Annie came back into the room, so she settled down on the couch with one of Ben's magazines. She had picked one at random from the pile on the floor. It was a psychiatric journal. She tried to read it, but she didn't understand most of the technical language. She thought about her father asking her if she knew what *paranoid* meant. He seemed to think they were still little kids.

She closed the magazine and stretched out on the sofa. She was tired from all that exercise with Flanagan. If Sherry was playing with him, she hoped she'd remember to latch the gate, although she didn't really think Flanagan would run far off, even if he did get out. He was getting used to his new home. When the Meyerses came home, she would invite Harriet over to play with him. She wasn't sure Sherry and Harriet would hit it off, but they might.

She was almost asleep when Cora spoke.

"This beats the toolshed all to smithereens," she said.

Annie jerked awake and smiled at her. "It's a nice little house, isn't it?"

"Had me a real bath. I must have stayed in that tub an hour. Myrt washed my hair. I can have another bath tonight if I want."

"That's nice. I like hot baths. They're relaxing."

"I got so relaxed, I nearly fell asleep. Might've drowned."

"Myrt wouldn't let you drown."

"She's a good woman, that Myrt."

"You bet. She's the best."

Cora was quiet so long, Annie though she had gone back to sleep. Then she said, "Can't stay here, though. It's not my house."

"Ben will find you a nice place when he gets back."

Cora didn't answer. She doesn't believe it, Annie thought. She doesn't trust us.

"Woman next door asked me if I was sick in the head," Cora said suddenly.

Oh, no! Annie thought. "Where did you see her?"

"I went out in the backyard while Myrt was taking

her shower. Woman leaned over the fence and asked me that."

"Well, she's a meddlesome woman," Annie said. "Pay no attention to her."

"I said, 'I'm likely saner than you are, lady. Why do you ask?' She said I was screaming in the night." Cora shook her head. "They used to say at the hospital I screamed in my sleep. How can I help what I do when I'm asleep?"

"You can't," Annie said. "Nobody can."

"She says, this neighbor woman, says, 'We got a nice quiet neighborhood here.' I says, 'Bully for you, lady.' And I came in the house." She looked around anxiously. "You seen my trophy? I don't know where I left it."

"I'll get it." Annie went into the room Cora was using for a bedroom and brought her the trophy. "It looks nice."

"Figure skating," Cora said. "That was my specialty. Boy! Was my mother proud of me!" She closed her eyes, and this time she did fall asleep. The trophy fell into her lap.

chapter 21

Annie sat on the back steps, waiting for Myrt to call. How wonderful it would be if the doctor said Cora could be cured completely. But she knew that was not likely.

Sherry and Flanagan were playing with his ball, racing up and down the drive, Sherry shrieking, Flanagan barking. Annie looked nervously toward the Andersons'.

The phone rang, and she ran inside to answer. It was Myrt.

"Dr. Ziegler just left. He was here a long time. I can talk because Cora's asleep."

"What did he say?" Annie dreaded to hear.

"Well, he says you can't diagnose a case like this in one visit. He went to the hospital yesterday to look up her records, but they weren't very well kept. There was no special doctor that looked after her case. Dr. Ziegler says he isn't much for labeling mental cases; says she obviously has manic-depressive symptoms and paranoia. He'll be back tomorrow."

"Can she get better?"

"Honey, these cases don't get better. What we can hope for is to find a medication that will give her a better life."

"Should I come over?"

"No, she'll sleep awhile. I'm going to put my feet up and watch some dumb game show on the tube."

"Mother will come all day tomorrow."

"Bless her heart. By the way, Ben called. I told him to quit worrying and catch his darned fish. Well, take it easy. I'll be in touch."

When Robert came home, Annie told him what Myrt had said.

"Where will she go when Ben comes back? Father's mad because she's over there."

"I don't know. Ben will find a place."

"Hey, I'm almost through my book, the one for the Kansas publisher."

"Great, Rob. What's the title?"

He grinned. "See how this grabs you: *Flanagan's Frolics*."

"It's about Flanagan?"

"Sort of. With embellishments. You gonna sue me?"

"It's terrific. He'll be famous. Do I get to read it?"

"No, but I'll show you the title page." He ran upstairs and came back with a sheet of typing paper, which he held out.

She read it aloud. " 'To Dog's best friend, my sister.' Me?"

"You. Okay?"

"Of course. I love it. Thanks!" She had never thought anyone would ever dedicate a book to her. "I hope it sells a million copies."

"I hope it gets accepted."

Sherry came in at the end of the conversation. "What are you guys talking about?"

"Robert's book."

"Am I in it?" Without waiting for an answer, she said, "I'm probably the prima ballerina." She twirled around the kitchen on her toes.

"Where's Flanagan?" Annie said. But Sherry had already danced outdoors and was tossing the ball for Flanagan, who caught it in his mouth.

Annie's mother drove into the yard, looking beautiful with her new haircut. She had an armful of packages. "I've been shopping for Cora. I hope I got the sizes right."

"You didn't tell me what Father said to the haircut."

"First total shock. But now he's decided I look like Carole Lombard."

"Whoever that is."

Sherry threw the ball in a high arc just as Annie came down the steps.

Next door, Mrs. Anderson was stooping over her flower bed, her back toward them.

The ball sailed over the hedge, bouncing close to Mrs. Anderson and then off into the grass. Before Annie could call out, Flanagan leaped the hedge and retrieved the ball. Mrs. Anderson screamed. Mr. Anderson rushed out of the house just in time to see Flanagan dash past his wife and jump the hedge again into his own yard.

"Did he bite you?" he yelled at his wife. "Did he attack you?"

Whatever she said was unintelligible. He stormed up to the hedge and shook his fist. "I am bringing this matter up at the special town meeting," he said. "That dog is a menace to the town, and I'm going to get rid of him if it's the last thing I do!"

Sherry screamed and burst into tears. Mrs. Anderson leaned on her husband, sobbing. Annie's father drove into the yard, got out of his wagon, and surveyed the scene.

"What now?" he said to Annie.

"All he did was go after his ball in their yard," Annie began.

"I'll sue!" Mr. Anderson shouted. "If my wife isn't safe in her own backyard, I'll take steps."

Annie's father sat down on the back steps and sighed. Flanagan rubbed his head against Father MacDougal's knee.

"Sherry," her father said, "stop that howling. Dog, I have nothing against you personally, but I'm beginning to think this town isn't big enough for you."

Annie put her arm around Flanagan's neck. She felt like screaming herself. "All he did was go into their yard to get his ball. He never touched that stupid woman."

Her father looked tired. "You recall in the New Testament that it says, 'The meek shall inherit the earth'? Sometimes I find myself wondering if that could be a mistranslation."

"You look exhausted," his wife said. "Where have you been?"

"I made a visit to the State Hospital for the Mentally Ill."

"Father!"

His wife looked at him closely. "Do you want to talk about it?"

"No." He got up and went into the house.

Annie was aghast. "He's been turning Cora in."

Her mother looked upset. "That's a very unkind conclusion to jump to about your father." And she, too, went inside.

"If he did," Annie said to Flanagan, "I'll never forgive him."

chapter 22

On her way back from her run in the meadow with Flanagan on Thursday, Annie stopped at Ben's to see how her mother was getting along with Cora.

She found her mother drinking a cup of coffee and reading a biography of William Faulkner. Cora was curled up at the end of the sofa, apparently asleep. She looked so small and thin in her new corduroy pants and her blue shirt, Annie felt an ache in her chest. In her too-big overcoat she had looked somehow stronger and tougher; now she looked so vulnerable.

"Is she asleep?"

Cora answered. "No, I'm not. It's those new pills. They make me groggy." Her eyes fluttered open. "Put me right out on a limbo."

Annie's mother smiled. "You just made a pun, Cora. 'Out on a limbo.' I like that."

"Glad you like it," Cora murmured, closing her eyes again. "You can keep it."

Annie was surprised. She had never heard Cora joke. If she was joking. She wondered if it was a good sign or a bad one. She looked at her mother, who said, "I like your friend Cora."

"Like you, too," Cora said. She opened her eyes. "You two related?"

"About as close as you can get," Annie's mother said. "She's my oldest child."

"Where's the rest of 'em?"

"One's in dancing class, one's teaching swimming, one's probably playing tennis. They're hard to keep track of."

"If it was me, I'd be skating," Cora said.

"Not yet," Annie's mother said. "No ice yet."

Annie listened to them in amazement. She had felt she had to be careful what she said to Cora, and Myrt talked to her in that nurse-to-patient manner. But her mother talked to her as if she were an old friend, and not a sick old friend, either. It made Cora respond more naturally, or maybe it was the new medication.

Flanagan had been lying obediently near the door where Annie had left him. Cora opened her eyes again and saw him. "There's your pony," she said. "Why doesn't he come over and say hello?"

"Flanagan—" Annie held out her hand, and he trotted

across the room to her, his nails clicking on Ben's bare floor. "Say hello to your friend Cora."

He gave Annie's mother an affectionate nudge and then stood beside Cora, wagging his tail.

"He remembers you," Annie said.

Cora shrank back a little. "Was he always that big?"

"You just didn't see him close up before. He likes you."

Cautiously, Cora reached out and patted his head. Flanagan pushed his head against her arm. She pulled back her hand. "I like him better when he's not so close."

Annie called Flanagan to her.

"It's not that I don't like him," Cora said.

"I know. He startles people, he's so big."

"What'd you say his name is?"

"Flanagan."

"No offense, Flanagan. You're a good dog." She closed her eyes and seemed really to go to sleep this time.

"Anything I can do?" Annie asked her mother quietly.

"No, dear. We're fine." She walked Annie and Flanagan to the door.

"She seems different," Annie said. "Better."

"Myrt says it's the new medicine. It makes her groggy, though. She sleeps most of the time."

"Well, I guess that's better than she was before."

The phone rang.

"I'll wait," Annie said. "It might be Ben."

The telephone was near the sofa where Cora lay. Annie's mother kept her voice low, but Annie saw Cora's eyelids flutter half open.

"Hello?" Her mother glanced at Annie and shook her head. It wasn't Ben. "This is Linda MacDougal. Father Vitale is away for a few days. Can I help you?"

Annie could hear the squawky sound of the voice on the other end. She saw her mother frown and glance at Cora, then turn her back to the sofa.

"I think you are unduly alarmed." Annie's mother's voice was so controlled and polite, Annie knew she was angry. It was the voice she used with some of the women in the church when they criticized her husband. "This is a temporary situation, and in any case, there is no problem whatsoever." She listened a moment. Annie saw her shoulders tense.

Cora's eyes were open now, and she was obviously listening.

"I really don't believe it is any concern of yours," Annie's mother said, and hung up. She said something under her breath.

"It was one of those women, wasn't it?" Cora said. "The neighbors. They been calling. I heard Myrt tell 'em off." She sat up. "It's me. People don't like to live next to crazy people."

"Cora . . ." Annie's mother sat down beside her and held her hand. "The troublemakers we have always with us. Don't give them a second thought."

"They'll make trouble for that nice young man. The priest, he says he is."

"Don't worry, Ben can handle them. He does it all the time."

"I've got to get out of here," Cora said. "I'll get you all in trouble."

"Take it easy. Nobody's going to get into trouble. Even if we did, it would be just another day. When you're part of a priest's family, a day without trouble is like a month in the country. Ben will have plans all worked out for you when he gets back. He's very good at that. Your job is to relax and feel better." She eased Cora back onto her pillows.

"People like me don't get well," Cora said. "That's what they told me at the hospital, all the time, a million times."

Annie said good-bye to Cora, and her mother followed her to the front steps. "I suppose that was the Felton woman?"

Her mother nodded. "I suppose mentally ill people really do frighten some people."

"Mother, I have to know what Father was doing at that hospital."

"No, you don't have to know any such thing."

"I have a right to know if he told them about Cora."

"He did not. And why don't you put a meat loaf together when you get home. Everything's there for it."

The Felton woman was leaning on the fence, staring at Annie and Flanagan. Annie stared back. Why couldn't people be a little bit kind? It wouldn't kill them, would it?

chapter 23

She asked herself that question again when she got home and found a notice in the mail from the town clerk, informing the owner of the Irish wolfhound registered as Ian Flanagan of Wild Rose Farm that the matter of the dog's potential and/or actual danger to the townspeople would be taken up at the town meeting on August 22.

Annie read it over several times. She had been expecting some ax to fall, after all that screaming business with the Andersons, but she had thought it would be another visit from Chief Porter, not a summons to the town meeting. "Oh, Flanagan," she said, "what are we going to do?" She wondered if she could take him to the town meeting so people would see how gentle he was. Probably dogs weren't allowed; only people—mean, hostile, meddling people.

Robert and Malcolm came in at the same time, and soon afterward one of the mothers brought Sherry home from her dancing class.

"Where's Mom?" Malcolm said. "What is there to eat? I think I'm beginning to psych out that serve of Ned's."

"You better hurry up," Robert said. "You haven't got much time left."

"Where's Mama?" Sherry said.

Robert looked closely at Annie's face. "What's wrong?"

She showed him the notice.

"They can't do that!" Malcolm said.

"They can and they will," Robert said. "We'd better start thinking."

"Do what?" Sherry tugged at Annie's arm. "Do what?"

"Oh, some mean people want to make us keep Flanagan locked up. Or even take him away from us."

"They can't do that!" Sherry sat down on the floor and threw her arms around Flanagan, who thought it was a game.

"We've got to marshal our forces," Robert said. "Think of everybody you know who's old enough to vote."

"Tell Mrs. Meyers," Sherry said.

Annie looked at her. "Sherry, you're a smart kid. I hadn't thought of that." If Mrs. Meyers was back from Maine at the time of the meeting, she would make a strong witness. If she wasn't, Mr. Thompson would probably do. Mr. Thompson could be very forceful.

She found the card Mrs. Meyers had given her and called the house number. The housekeeper said Mrs. Meyers was not expected back until after Labor Day. She tried Mr. Thompson's number at the kennel, but there was no answer. She'd try him later. If she got all her forces organized, with the boys helping, at least the Andersons and Mrs. Hanson and whoever else was complaining would have some people to contend with.

She found her father in his study and told him about the notice, knowing she couldn't avoid telling him, since it would probably be in the paper, and that stupid editor would think he had had the last laugh.

Her father heard her without comment. He looked at Flanagan, who was sitting beside her as if he were listening attentively to everything she said. Suddenly Flanagan snapped his head forward and clicked his jaws. Her father pulled back.

"He's only trying to catch a fly," Annie said. It was discouraging that her own father reacted that way to Flanagan. "If that had been Bingo trying to catch a fly, you'd have thought it was cute."

"Flanagan is too big to be cute," her father said. "That's the problem. When he acts like a normal dog, people take it as a threat. Well, Daughter, I'll speak to Paul Jansen. He's still town moderator, isn't he? I haven't been to a town meeting in some time."

"Yes, he's moderator, but that's only like a sort of chairman, isn't it? I mean, what can he do? I thought if Mrs. Meyers were there . . . but she won't be back till after Labor Day. Maybe Mr. Thompson would come."

"Good idea. Well, you'll have to attend to all this. We did agree that the dog was to be your responsibility."

"I couldn't keep him penned up in the run all the time. That would be cruel. He's a big dog; he needs exercise."

"Why not wait till you know what you have to deal with before you start imagining horrible fates. Meanwhile, we will pray for Flanagan, and you must brace yourself for whatever is to come."

She left the study feeling angry. A big help Father was.

"What did he say?" Robert asked.

"Pray," she said bitterly.

Robert grinned. "That's our dad. Well, Mom just drove in. She believes in pray and *do*."

Her mother listened while she made the meat loaf and put it in the oven, then scrubbed some baking potatoes.

"I'm sorry about the meat loaf," Annie said. "I got distracted."

"It's all right. I'm early, anyway. Myrt came back. Look, try not to get into a swivet about this. I'll contact all the people I can think of to put in a good word for Flanagan." She patted him as he came to her at the sound of his name. "And now you go out on the porch, old boy, while I'm cooking dinner. That's the rule."

"I'll take him out," Sherry said.

"You'll go take a shower and get into normal clothes, my little ballerina."

A little later Annie's mother came out and sat beside Annie on the back steps. Flanagan was bringing sticks and laying them at Annie's feet. She threw them for him, but she was feeling depressed.

"Your friend Cora," her mother said. "She breaks one's heart."

"Yes. That's what Myrt said. And I guess she does. You keep thinking of how she would have been if that awful thing hadn't happened to her."

"I kept thinking of her mother. How it would feel to have your child lost to you in that way." She was silent for a minute. "Myrt thinks the new medicine is causing a lot of depression. She just sat on the sofa all the time I was there. I kept thinking she was asleep, but then she would move or say something. She ate hardly any lunch."

"Maybe it can be adjusted. The medication."

"Myrt is trying to figure out if she could take her in at her apartment until Benny comes up with something, but there are problems. Her landlady is a fussbudget."

"Those neighbors of Benny's . . ."

"I know. As they say—'I'm sorry for the homeless and the sick, but don't bring them anywhere near me.' Ben's even been getting complaints about the music the boys play at the school. 'Too loud,' they say, when their own kids are bringing down the walls with their stereos. Well—" She changed her tone and stood up. "The way of the world is the way of the world. I'd better check the meat loaf."

chapter 24

Annie had planned to take Flanagan out to the meadow again on Friday, but when she woke up, it was raining. She dressed, fed Flanagan, and brought him into the kitchen. Her mother was working in her studio, and her father's study door was closed.

"Tell Mom I'm going to the Y," Malcolm said on his way out.

She heard Robert's typewriter and wondered what he was working on, now that he had finished his book.

The telephone rang. She picked up the kitchen extension and heard her mother already answering. It was Myrt's voice on the other end. She sounded very upset.

"Linda," she was saying, "this is Myrt. Cora has disappeared."

"Disappeared!" Annie said. "Are you sure?"

"What happened, Myrt?" Annie's mother said.

"She seemed so tired last night, I thought she was sleeping late. I slept late myself; it's the first night we haven't been up a lot. When I decided I'd better check on her, she was gone." Myrt sounded close to tears.

"Did she take her things?" Annie's mind was jumping from one possibility to another.

"No, just what she had on—those jeans you got her, Linda, and the shirt and sweater."

"Maybe she just went out for a walk," Annie's mother said.

"In the rain? With no breakfast? Ben called just a few minutes after I found her gone. He's on his way home. He said to call Bernie Porter and Annie. I already called Bernie."

"Did she take her skating trophy?" Annie asked.

"I didn't notice. I was so upset."

"Would you mind looking?"

"All right. Hold on."

Her mother hung up her extension and came into the kitchen. "Why do you want to know that?"

"She's never without it. If she wasn't coming back, she'd take it."

"Wouldn't she take clothes and things, too?"

"If she was upset, she could forget them. She wouldn't forget the trophy. It's like her real self."

Robert came into the kitchen. "What's up?"

"Cora's disappeared."

Myrt came back on the line. "The trophy is there, and

there's a note under it. It was folded up real small and I never saw it."

"What does it say?"

"It says: 'Thanks. Nice folks. Give trophy to girl and dog.' "

"That's it?"

"That's it. And Annie . . ."

"What?"

"Her bottle of pills is gone."

"Myrt, if you can get hold of Chief Porter, ask him if he'll meet me at the arboretum. And why don't you stay there, in case she comes back?"

After she hung up, she repeated what Myrt had said. Her mother was already getting her raincoat. "I'll drive you out there."

"I'll go, too." Robert grabbed two parkas from the back hall hooks and tossed one to Annie.

"We have to take Flanagan," Annie said. "He can find her faster than we can."

They went in the station wagon, Annie's mother driving fast and expertly. None of them spoke.

Annie sat in the back with her arms around Flanagan, thinking of all the things she wished she had done. She should have offered to sleep at Ben's so Myrt wouldn't have to be watching over Cora night and day. Why hadn't she thought of it? She wished she had spent more time with Cora yesterday, trying to cheer her up.

Chief Porter's car was pulling into the side of the road at the arboretum entrance when they got there. Annie's mother parked just behind him.

Annie told him about the note and the missing pills. "I'm going to look in the toolshed." She started running down the path, Flanagan dashing ahead of her, enjoying being back in his familiar woods. The light rain blew in their faces. Annie's heart pounded. She wished she knew how long Cora had been gone. And how long would it take for those pills to kill a person? Or would they kill? Maybe she would just get very sick to her stomach.

She turned so fast into the path to the toolshed, she stumbled against Flanagan and nearly fell down. He got to the shed first and barked at the closed door. Annie pulled on the old door. It was stuck.

Robert caught up with her and helped to pull. The door jerked open.

It was cold and dark in the toolshed. Flanagan nosed around it eagerly, sniffing in every corner. Cora was not there.

In a few minutes Chief Porter joined them, breathing hard, and Annie's mother came up behind him. The chief unhooked a flashlight from his belt and beamed it around the shed. The place still smelled of cheap wine.

In a corner Robert found the empty prescription bottle. He held it up.

"Oh, no," Annie's mother said softly.

"She can't be far off," Chief Porter said. "Let's fan out and hunt. She'll need to get to the hospital fast if she's been taking those pills." He walked down the path, turning left at the intersection.

Annie's mother took the same path to the right. Robert went around to the back of the toolshed, climbing the incline.

Annie put her hand on Flanagan's head. "Find Cora, Flanagan."

But Flanagan's attention was caught by a chipmunk swaying on a pine branch just beyond his reach. He barked and jumped up, and the chipmunk scampered farther up the tree.

Annie stood still, trying to think where Cora would go. She must still have the wine bottle with her. Probably she bought it on the way over here, to help her swallow the pills. And alcohol hastened the action of medicine, didn't it? She might have taken some of the pills and put the rest in her pocket, to go somewhere else, knowing that Annie would look for her here first.

"Flanagan, stop barking. Help me find Cora." She pushed at him, and he looked at her questioningly. She took him inside the shed again for a minute, so he would pick up Cora's scent. Wasn't that how they did it on TV? "Now. Find Cora."

She led him outside, and he trotted off in the direction of the river. The river! What if she went to the river to finish off the pills, so in case they didn't work, she could drown herself? Annie broke into a run, Flanagan keeping just ahead of her.

She passed Chief Porter making a search of both sides of the path, wherever there was enough space to allow a person in.

"Flanagan's heading for the river," she said.

"Right behind you." Chief Porter came out of the brush and followed her.

Cora hadn't quite made it. Flanagan found her sprawled on the wet ground within half a dozen yards of the riverbank.

Annie went down on her knees beside her, feeling for Cora's pulse. Cora's hand was icy cold, and the pulse was so faint she thought at first that there wasn't any.

She moved back to let Chief Porter examine her. Robert caught up with them.

"Flanagan found her."

"Still alive?"

"Just.

Chief Porter lifted Cora. "Got to get to the hospital fast as we can."

"Find Mother," Annie said to Robert. She went ahead of the chief, parting wet branches out of his way.

Her mother and Robert arrived at the cars just minutes after Annie and the chief got there. He put Cora on the backseat of the patrol car. Annie got in beside her and held her head in her lap. "Flanagan, you go with Robert," she said.

As soon as they got out of the back roads, the chief put on the siren. Annie glanced back and saw her mother right behind them. She wouldn't have thought the old wagon could go so fast.

She kept taking Cora's pulse. It seemed to get fainter, and her face was yellow. Once she jerked violently.

"Cora, Cora," Annie whispered. "Don't die. Please don't die. We'll take care of you."

Chief Porter's brakes screamed as he swerved in at the hospital emergency entrance, and in minutes Cora had been transferred to a gurney and whisked inside. The chief gave the admitting clerk the necessary information while Annie and her mother waited near the door. Robert was walking Flanagan in the driveway.

"There's nothing more we can do," Chief Porter said when he joined them.

"Can they save her?" Annie asked him.

"They're sure going to try." He put his hand on her shoulder. "You're white as a ghost, child. Go home and get some rest." As he turned her toward the door, he said, "They say she wouldn't have had a chance if you hadn't found her when you did."

"It was Flanagan found her."

When they got home, Benny was there, waiting to hear. He looked strained and pale. "My mother and I had just worked out a plan," he said. "That was what I called Myrt to tell Cora. My mother lives alone now. She said she'd love to take Cora; it would give her something to do."

"It wouldn't be easy," Annie's mother said.

"My mother never looks for the easy stuff. She's no nurse, but she got all of us through dozens of illnesses." He was pacing the floor.

"Ben, relax," Annie's mother said gently. "They're doing all they can. Let me make you some coffee."

He shook his head. "I blame myself for going off without getting her better settled."

"How could she have been better settled?"

"Well, you know about those good Christian neighbors of mine, who don't want anybody *different* in the neighborhood. They think anyone with any kind of mental illness is a violent, raving lunatic. Well, I left Mom at the church; I'll go take her home. Dougal is down there, too. He said to tell you he'd stop by the hospital on his way home." He hugged Annie. "Bless you and your beautiful monster of a dog."

When he had gone, Annie's mother said, "Would you children like something hot to drink? Why don't you get into some dry clothes and come back. What would you like—cocoa?"

"How about," Robert said, "that coffee you make for Father with whipped cream on top?"

She smiled. "You're too young for coffee, but this is a special moment. You, too, Annie?"

"Please." Annie got some hamburger and put it in a dish for Flanagan. Then she went upstairs to change her clothes. One sentence kept running through her mind over and over. "Cora, Cora, Cora, hang in there."

chapter 25

Annie called the hospital as soon as she woke up the next morning. Cora was alive but still unconscious.

When she came downstairs, her father was just coming in, looking tired. He had spent the night at the hospital, which surprised her.

"What do the doctors say?"

"The resident, Dr. Snow, was worried during the night. But this morning her vital signs have improved. He says he doesn't want to go out on a limb, but his guess is that she'll pull through. It remains to be seen whether it's damaged her mental processes any more than they already were." He leaned down and patted Flanagan. "You and Annie were heroes, old boy."

Robert came into the room in time to hear his last remark. "It's going to make a difference."

"What difference?" Annie said.

"At the town meeting."

"Don't count on that," his father said. "Nobody knew Cora, and I'm afraid there isn't much compassion among a lot of people for someone they don't know."

"Especially if she's crazy," Robert said. "That's right. But somehow . . ." He went back upstairs, a thoughtful look on his face.

"I'm going to catch some sleep," Annie's father said. "If there's any news, call me."

Malcolm came downstairs looking sleepy. "Is that lady still alive?"

Annie nodded.

"My friend Ned's father thinks she'll pull through okay."

"How does your friend Ned's father know?"

"Well, he's a neurologist." He found the cereal box he wanted and poured some into a bowl. "Our big match is only four days away, in case anybody remembers."

"I'd forgotten. So much has been happening."

"I know. We're upstaged."

"Are you going to beat your friend this time?"

"You bet. I've got his serve psyched out. I'm going to massa-cree him. After the match his folks are going to take us to the Clam Shack for dinner."

It seemed to Annie like a long morning, waiting for news. She walked Flanagan in the yard, and later Sherry played ball with him, but in his run, to avoid any chance of outraging the Andersons again. They had managed to be outside watching all the comings and goings yesterday. Now as Annie started toward the house, Mr. Anderson leaned over the hedge with an unpleasant smile and said, "Enjoy your dog while you still can."

If she'd needed any clue as to who had filed the complaint with the selectmen, this was it. She stopped and faced him. "Mr. Anderson, is it fun to be mean?"

His mouth fell open. She went in and slammed the door.

Robert came running downstairs with some typed sheets in his hand.

"New story?" She was trying to calm down.

"Nonfiction." He ran out the door.

The house was quiet: her father asleep upstairs, her mother making the last summer deliveries to the gift shops, Sherry at dancing class. She tried to think clearly about Benny's mother taking Cora. Would it work? Mrs. Vitale was in her sixties, but she seemed young and energetic, and she was a cheerful, positive person, probably the best kind of person Cora could have. Ben would keep an eye on things to make sure it wasn't too much for his mother.

Later in the afternoon Benny stopped by to tell her that Cora had regained consciousness. "She doesn't remember anything that happened, and she doesn't know us, but the doctor said that wasn't surprising." He sprawled in a chair. "I'm beat. She's still wearing your ID bracelet. That really confused people."

"She can keep it if she wants to."

"Did you know your brothers are downtown conducting a poll?"

"You're kidding. What kind of poll?"

"The question is, 'Do you believe that Annie MacDougal's dog should be: (*a*) confined to his run; (*b*) sent away; (*c*) allowed to live a normal life; or (*d*) none of the above.' "

"Oh, no!"

"Rob is stationed in front of the IGA, and Malcolm is in front of Hanson's ice-cream parlor. They're very serious and businesslike about it."

"Do people pay any attention to them?"

"Quite a few. I watched for a few minutes. Some people laugh, some are annoyed at being waylaid, some seem to take it quite seriously. The news is out, of course, that Jack Anderson is going to get you at the town meeting. Sherry is the backup. She keeps them supplied with sharp pencils."

"She's supposed to be at dancing class." She looked at the clock.

"She was on her way home, Rob said, and she saw them. Of course she had to get in on the act." He finished his coffee. "Well, I've got a million things to do."

"Do you think I could go see Cora?"

"Better wait and get your mother to take you. They might not let you in alone. Visiting hours are two to four." He got up, stepping over Flanagan, who was lying across his feet. "Take it easy, friends."

Annie wanted to take Flanagan for a walk, but she didn't want to go through town to the meadow. It seemed like the best idea to keep Flanagan out of the public eye until the town meeting. "You might do something impetuous," she said to him, "like one of your leaps that knocks over rows and rows of small children. Oh, Flanagan." She put her arms around his neck. "If they try to take you away from me, I won't allow it. I'll picket town hall. I'll bring suit or something." She thought of Mr. Thompson and called his number at the kennel, but again there was no answer.

She decided to walk Flanagan up the road at least as far as the turnoff into the arboretum road. She did not want to go into the arboretum itself. "I'm not sure I ever want to go there again," she said.

She let Flanagan run alongside her unleashed. He was much better about staying close to her than he had been. At the Sanderses' house the little girl ran out to pat him, and he gave her a wet kiss on her cheek. She laughed with delight.

"My dad is going to the town meeting," she said, "to vote for your dog."

"Oh, that's nice. Tell him thanks."

The closer the town meeting got, the more Annie worried. It was going to be so awful to hear Mr. Anderson and probably Mrs. Hanson, and who knew who else, standing up and talking against Flanagan as if he were some kind of four-legged atom bomb. And what if they won?

When she got home, Sherry and the boys were there. Robert and Malcolm were studying a computer printout. Robert waved it at her. "We took a poll."

"I heard," Annie said.

"Here's how it came out," Robert said. "(*a*) Confined to his run, thirteen; (*b*) sent away, four; (*c*) allowed to live a normal life, twenty-two; (*d*) None of the above, two. Margin for error, three to five percent."

"Were people serious, or were they just playing along?"

"A lot of them were serious."

"Then it comes out seventeen against, twenty-two for, two uncommitted."

"And that's too close for comfort," Malcolm said. "But Rob has a secret weapon. He won't tell me what it is."

"It has to be a total surprise or it won't work," Robert said. "Listen, Annie, tomorrow morning a guy is going to take some pictures of Flanagan. Don't fight it, okay?"

"What for?" Annie said, frowning.

"Trust me. Just let him do it."

"Who is he?"

"Don't worry about it. Just do what he asks."

"Rob, you aren't going to get me into more trouble, are you?"

"Annie!" He looked hurt. "Did I ever let you down?"

"Well, no."

"So trust me."

"All right," she said. "It can't be much worse than it is already."

chapter 26

The next day Annie's mother came home from a guild luncheon seething with anger. "Those women!" she said.

"What women?" Annie said. "Benny called. Cora didn't recognize him. She doesn't remember any of us."

"Well." Her mother sat down. "That may wear off."

"What women are you mad at?"

"Myra Evans, Jennie Parsons, Helen Ashley . . . telling me, ever so tactfully, ever so helpfully, that we really ought to get rid of 'that dog' before he causes embarrassment for your father."

"Even Mrs. Ashley?"

"Well, she's related to the Hansons. I suppose that

young Hanson woman told her her wild tale. Oh, they are so mealymouthed, they make me sick."

"I really don't get it," Annie said. "Flanagan never did any of them any harm, or anybody else."

"I think it's jealousy. They all long to be a buddy of Mrs. Meyers."

"Why?"

"Because she's a very wealthy woman. They're snobs. I'm afraid I lost my temper. In a nice way, of course—that nasty-nice way that they use. Your father always says that any person in a public position—a priest, a doctor, whatever—is a target for malice. He's right."

Annie pulled Flanagan close to her. "I don't want to make trouble for Father."

Just then her father came into the room. "Don't worry about trouble for your father," he said. "He's used to it."

"Tell me the truth, Father. Do you want me to give Flanagan back to Mrs. Meyers?"

"Indeed I do not," he said. "The dog has done no harm to anyone. He's a fine dog. My parishioners are not going to dictate to me about my family's private lives." He reached down and patted Flanagan. "You make me sneeze, but I like you. Annie, there's a man in the yard with a camera. He says he wants to see you."

"Oh, heavens, what for?" her mother said.

"I don't know," Annie said, "but Robert arranged it, and he said to trust him." She took hold of Flanagan's collar. "I think it has to do with Flanagan. Come on, boy."

Sherry whirled into the room. "A man just took my picture doing a pirouette!"

"I suppose you asked him to," Annie said.

"Of course." She danced around the room. "Maybe it'll be in the paper."

"Probably the *New York Times*," her father said. "Front page."

"Really?" Sherry said.

Annie went out to the yard and found a tall young man with camera equipment. "I'm Annie MacDougal," she said.

"And don't tell me, let me guess—that's Flanagan. Can I get a full-face picture of him, standing alone?"

"Flanagan, stay," Annie said. She had seen this man before. He was from the *Chronicle*. What was Robert up to?

Flanagan stayed, but he was sitting.

"No, stand up." She nudged him into a standing position.

"Stand over here so he'll be looking toward you," the man said.

She was conscious of Mrs. Anderson watching them from next door. Annie felt like giggling. The whole thing was so crazy. If she hadn't been afraid of losing Flanagan, she would have laughed it all off. Grown-ups behaving like little kids, out of a mixed-up mess of their own meannesses and vanities. When you took it apart and looked at it, it really had nothing to do with Flanagan. That group her mother had been so angry with today was always criticizing her father one way or another: He was too Low Church, or he was too High Church, or his sermons were dull, or his sermons were too intellectual. He was convinced they'd get rid of him if they could. Benny, too.

She posed with her hand on Flanagan's neck, then

tossed Flanagan's ball so the photographer could get a picture of him jumping. That one took several shots.

Finally he said, "Okay, thanks a lot," and was gone.

"I don't know," she said to Flanagan, "whether you're going to be famous or infamous, but you're going to be well known."

Flanagan dropped his ball at her feet, and she tossed it for him. Mrs. Anderson still watched. Then as the ball bounced near the hedge, she scuttled into the house.

As Annie took Flanagan into the house finally, she wondered if Mr. Endicott would really print a picture of Flanagan, especially after that visit she and Benny had paid him. And what would he say in the paper? She hoped Robert knew what he was doing.

"Mr. Thompson called," her mother said. "He just heard about the town meeting. He said to tell you he'll be there with bells on. He's in a fine rage."

"Good," Annie said. "I tried to call him. I wish Mrs. Meyers were here, but she won't be back till next week."

"I should tell you that some of the women stood up for Flanagan. May Sheldon, Sally Roberts, and Jo Ainsley were the most vocal. Especially Jo."

"They're the nicest, anyway. Mom, when can we go to see Cora?"

"Ben said to wait another day. She's still very groggy, and she doesn't recognize anyone."

"I was there this morning," her father said, looking up from his paper. "Ben's right. Wait a bit."

"Father, is she going to be all right? I mean, you know, as all right as she can be?"

"The doctor says it's too soon to tell. She might never

be any better than she is right now, she might die, or she might improve. I'll ask prayers for her on Sunday."

Annie didn't say so, but she was wondering how many people in town would really pray for Cora, or, in fact, who even knew she existed. People shouldn't get lost like that.

She heard Robert come into the kitchen and make a phone call. When she went out there, he was saying, "Thanks a lot. And don't forget the byline."

"Robert, what are you up to?" she said.

"My best." He grinned. "Has it occurred to you that school starts in exactly nine days?"

Annie groaned.

chapter 27

Annie and her mother went the next afternoon to see Cora.

"There hasn't been any change," the nurse told them. "She won't know you."

Annie was shocked when she saw Cora; she looked so small and thin in the hospital bed.

"The doctor had a scan done," the nurse said. "No evidence of anything wrong there, no tumor or anything."

Annie wished she wouldn't talk about Cora in front of her. Cora opened her eyes and looked at them dully, with no apparent recognition. Annie took her small, cold hand in hers.

"Hi, Cora. How you feeling?"

"Fine," Cora said.

"She always says that," the nurse said. "It doesn't mean anything."

Annie wanted to say "Please go away," but of course she couldn't. "We brought you some flowers. Can you see them?"

The nurse had put them in a vase on Cora's little bedside table.

"I see them," Cora said.

"Say thank you to the nice ladies," the nurse said.

Annie wanted to slug her.

"Thank you," Cora muttered.

It was hard to think of things to say. Annie's mother said a few things, like how glad they were that Cora felt better, and how nice it would be when she could leave the hospital. Cora made no answer to anything.

"It's not much use," the nurse said. "I'll get her some ginger ale. It's time for her to take some liquids." Briskly she left the room.

Annie and her mother exchanged glances.

"We'd better go," her mother said.

Annie held Cora's hand tight in both of hers. "Get well quick, Cora," she said. She leaned over and kissed her forehead. Cora smelled of hospital soap.

When they were almost at the door, Cora said, "Why didn't you bring your pony?"

Annie whirled around. "You do remember!" She went back and put her hand on Cora's arm. "You know me, don't you?"

"Sure. The girl." She closed her eyes.

"Cora, everything's going to be all right!"

In the hall they found Benny coming for a visit. Excitedly Annie told him about Cora's recognition. His face lit up.

"I'll tell the doctor. That's great! Maybe now's the time to tell her about living with my mom, so she won't be worrying."

Annie felt as if one big load had been lifted off their shoulders. "Wait till I tell Flanagan," she said. "He was the one she remembered first."

chapter 28

Annie had never been to a town meeting before, so she didn't know whether it was an unusually large crowd or not, but there seemed to be a great many people there. She and her family sat in the second row. Benny wasn't in sight, but she knew he would be there in time for the discussion of Annie's dog. It was scheduled last, after the other warrants.

She had expected to be bored by the arguments about sewer systems and abutments and all that, and part of the time she was, but it was interesting to hear people arguing so passionately about things that didn't seem all that important. Maybe they really were, and she just didn't understand them. Jack Anderson, she noticed, was loudly against everything. Mrs. Anderson didn't speak, but she smiled triumphantly every time Jack spoke.

Mr. Jansen, the town moderator, was patient but firm, insisting on proper parliamentary procedures.

Robert kept looking at the big clock over the podium and craning his neck to look toward the back. Malcolm was reading a science-fiction paperback. Sherry, who had insisted on coming, had fallen asleep with her head on her mother's shoulder. Only Flanagan, Annie thought, was at home alone, Flanagan, the star of the show.

She studied the faces of the people, trying to guess who would be for Flanagan and who against him. She noticed Todd Bethel and his parents, and she wondered how old you had to be to vote. Todd was seventeen.

Malcolm had pointed out his friend Ned and his father, but they couldn't vote because they lived out of town. It was nice of them to come, though.

As the evening wore on, the anxiety that Annie had been trying to control began to mount. It was hard to sit still and listen to arguments about somebody's garage annex when Flanagan's fate was coming up soon.

She heard the door at the back of the hall open and close. She half turned to see who it was, hoping it was Benny, but it was Mrs. Meyers and Harriet. She was really surprised. They sat next to Mr. Thompson near the back. Annie felt better having them there. Could they have come from Maine on purpose to speak for Flanagan?

Robert saw them and nodded at her, making a circle of his thumb and forefinger. He looked at the clock every couple of minutes now. She was sure he was looking for Benny.

She turned her attention to the meeting again as Mr. Jansen told Jack Anderson he was out of order. Mr. Jansen sat in the middle of a long table with the board of selectmen on either side of him. The town clerk sat beside them at a small table, taking notes on one of those little machines that court stenographers use.

Suddenly, to her amazement, Benny appeared at the back of the stage, coming in through one of the side doors. He tiptoed over to Mr. Jansen and put a folded sheet of paper in front of him. Mr. Jansen nodded and Benny disappeared. Robert smiled and relaxed. He scribbled on a scrap of paper and showed it to her. He had written, "Not to worry."

His father, sitting next to Annie, leaned over and read the note, raised his eyebrows, and, as Annie looked at him questioningly, shook his head. Whatever was going on seemed to be strictly a Benny-Robert plot. She tried hard not to worry, but when she heard Jack Anderson's raucous voice and saw the smug faces of people like Mrs. Evans and Mrs. Parsons, and the indifference of many others, it was not easy. The younger Hansons were there, she noticed, but not the older Mr. Hanson, the ice-cream man who had laughed when Todd told him about his daughter-in-law's complaints. Nobody seemed to want to meet her glance.

A vote was taken on Joe LeBaron's garage addition. He lost.

The next and last item on the agenda was Annie MacDougal's dog. She looked at Jack Anderson and saw the expectant smile on his face. She noticed that Mrs. Anderson's wrist was bandaged; were they going to have the nerve to claim Flanagan had bitten her?

Mr. Jansen read the complaint: ". . . excessive barking, dangerous behavior around small children, trespassing, frightening and behaving in a threatening manner on a neighbor's lawn . . ." There were sixteen names attached to the petition. Annie was shocked. Some of those people, she was sure, had never laid eyes on Flanagan.

Her mother reached for her hand and held it tight while various people voiced their complaints: Jack Anderson first, then his wife claiming to have been "menaced," then the younger Mrs. Hanson and some of her neighbors who "feared for their children's right to play on the street in safety."

Annie listened in a daze.

Then Todd Bethel asked for the floor. He told what he had seen: "A big dog, not much more than a puppy, trying to play ball with some kids. A friendly dog. A perfectly nice, gentle dog."

Mr. Sanders was on his feet, telling about the times he had seen and talked to Annie and her dog, how much his eight-year-old thought of Flanagan.

Arguments flew back and forth, claims and counterclaims. Mr. Jansen had trouble keeping order. Annie stared hard at the big portrait of George Washington that hung on the back wall, trying not to scream at them all.

Then a familiar voice spoke from the back of the hall. Annie turned quickly. Mrs. Meyers was speaking; Harriet and Mr. Thompson were sitting beside her.

Her voice was calm, almost quiet, but she looked very angry. "I have come down from Maine especially for this meeting," she said. "The dog you are discussing in such extraordinary terms comes from my kennels. He was a favorite of my daughter's. I helped Mr. Thompson train him. Like all Irish wolfhounds that I have ever encountered, he is a gentle, sweet-tempered, playful dog. I'm sure Annie MacDougal has found him so. I should just like to say that if this meeting passes any kind of condemnation of that dog, whether to force restraint upon him or exile, I shall bring suit." She sat down.

There was a dead silence. Annie wanted to cheer, but within moments she knew the speech had been a mistake.

Behind Annie a woman murmured, "Who does she think she is?"

They resented Mrs. Meyers—her money, her threat to sue, her power. Annie could feel it all over the room.

"Well," Mr. Jansen said in his most uncontroversial voice, "we hope nothing so drastic will occur. Perhaps this is the moment when I should tell you about a story coming out in tomorrow's *Chronicle*. I have here an early edition of the front page." He held it up, although no one but the selectmen could see it clearly.

"Take a vote," Jack Anderson yelled.

"Just a moment, Jack. You are out of order. There is a large picture on the front page of the dog we have been discussing. The caption beneath it reads: MONSTER OR HERO?" He held up his hand as a murmur ran through the crowd. "The story is not long. I would like to read it." He cleared his throat.

Annie looked at Robert, a what's-going-on look. He winked.

Mr. Jansen started to read. " 'A woman named Cora Hardy and a dog named Flanagan came to our town at about the same time. They had never met, but Flanagan was destined to save Cora Hardy's life, not once but twice.' "

Annie's hands were shaking so badly she had to clasp them tightly together.

The story went on, telling briefly how Flanagan had first found Cora alone and ill in the arboretum toolshed, and how Annie had looked after her in the near hurricane, and how he found her again when despair had overcome her and she had tried to kill herself. " 'Cora Hardy, who at eighteen won a trophy for figure skating, had spent twenty terrible years in our state mental institution. Flanagan, too, was "different," an Irish wolfhound, the biggest breed of dog. Because they were not exactly like everybody else, both of them were threatened and persecuted. Each of them is a kind and loving creature. Have we in this town forgotten how to care?' " Slowly, without looking at the crowd, Mr. Jansen folded the paper and laid it on the table. There wasn't a sound in the hall.

Todd Bethel's father stood up. "I move the complaint about Annie MacDougal's dog be struck from the agenda."

"Second the motion." It was Mr. Thompson's voice, sounding loud and fierce.

"All those in favor?"

There was a roar of "ayes."

"Opposed?"

Jack Anderson opened his mouth and closed it again.

"Jack, this was your petition. Do you accept the vote?" Mr. Jansen asked.

Jack Anderson made a mumbling sound that could have been yes.

"Then it is so ordered that the complaint be dismissed."

The applause woke Sherry. "Is Flanagan safe?" she said.

"He's safe!" Annie said. "He's safe."

chapter 29

Father MacDougal leaned his elbows on the pulpit and took off his glasses. The youth choir was singing, so Robert and Annie were in the choir stalls, Benny sitting in the chair at the end of the stalls. Malcolm was seated near the altar in his acolyte vestments, looking, Annie thought, as if he were still replaying in his mind the seven-set match he had won from his friend Ned.

"I want to talk to you about something that is, in a sense, personal," Father MacDougal said. "As you know, I avoid getting personal in my addresses to you, but this is important to me." He paused and cleaned his glasses. He was talking without notes. "For one thing, it involves my admitting that I was at least to some extent wrong." He gave them his rare smile. "And it is very hard for a Scot to admit he is wrong."

Annie and Robert exchanged glances. Robert shrugged and shook his head. He didn't know what was coming, either. Annie could see her mother's face. She, too, looked surprised.

"Father Vitale and I," her father went on, "have had a running battle for a long time about how much of our resources should go to social causes, how much retained in our own parish. I am sure most of you know I was opposed to the social causes, especially outside our own bailiwick." He took a sip from the glass of water on the shelf of the pulpit.

Whatever it is, Annie thought, it's hard for him to say it.

"Because of certain circumstances that have arisen recently, I had occasion to visit our mental hospital. I went, frankly, out of curiosity. I wanted to see for myself. I have been back several times." His voice was suddenly more emotional than Annie could remember hearing it. "The place is appalling. Ten or twelve ill people are jammed into rooms intended for four. It was built to house four hundred and fifty people; it now has over two thousand. The main building was gutted by fire eight years ago and never repaired. There is no occupational therapy, no entertainment, *nothing* for those poor souls to do but chain-smoke and sit. Many of them have been turned loose with no resources at all." His voice rose. "It is appalling! It is Bedlam all over again."

He took another sip of water and spoke more calmly.

"And so I am going to propose to you and to the vestry that under Father Vitale's expert guidance we put together a plan to see if we can make some small dent in that terrible situation." He raised his hand in the sign of the cross and said, " 'Grace be unto you, and peace, from God our Father, and from the Lord Jesus Christ.' "

He turned abruptly away and came down from the pulpit as the crowd murmured its surprised "Amens."

Annie looked at her mother's face again and saw the tenderness with which she watched her husband move back to the altar. She looked at Benny and saw tears in his eyes. She had never, she thought, loved her father so much.

As the choir stood to sing the anthem during the collection, she thought, I never knew him. He grew up in another country, he loved a woman I never knew and married her and watched her long, painful death. He had a whole life long before I was born.

Malcolm rode home with Mother after church, but Annie and Robert chose to walk. They talked about everything except their father's short sermon.

"I had to fight that guy at the *Chronicle* to get a byline on Flanagan's story," Robert said, "but I got it." He grinned. "It'll look great on my résumé."

"I hope he paid you."

"Not yet, but he will. Ben will see to that. Ben edited the story; he was a terrific help."

Annie pointed to a new sign stuck on a stake by the side of the road: VOTE FOR JACK ANDERSON FOR PLANNING COMMISSIONER.

Robert laughed. "If at first you don't succeed . . ."

As they turned into their driveway, Flanagan began to bark joyously. As if by a mutual impulse Annie and Robert stopped.

"What did you think of it?" she said.

"Father's had a Learning Experience."

"No, seriously."

"Seriously, I wanted to jump into the pulpit and hug him."

"Me, too. I almost cried."

"The best thing was, he wasn't eloquent."

Annie nodded. She knew what he meant.

Robert pushed his glasses up on his forehead. "I guess this sounds pretty gooey," he said, "but I'll say it, anyway: I think our family is really neat."

Annie smiled. "It's a touch gooey, but I'll go along with it." She shouted to Flanagan, who had his front paws on the chain-link fence, barking indignantly. "Hang in there, Flanagan. I'm coming."